LOVE'S BOUNTY

What Reviewers Say About
Yolanda Wallace's Work

The War Within

"*The War Within* has a masterpiece quality to it. It's a story of the heart told with heart—a story to be savored—and proof that you're never too old to find (or rediscover) true love."
—*Lambda Literary*

Rum Spring

"The writing was possibly the best I've seen for the modern lesfic genre, and the premise and setting was intriguing. I would recommend this one."—*The Lesbrary*

Murphys's Law

"Prepare to be thrilled by a love story filled with high adventure as they move toward an ending as turbulent as the weather on a Himalayan peak."—*Lambda Literary*

Visit us at www.boldstrokesbooks.com

By the Author

In Medias Res

Rum Spring

Lucky Loser

Month of Sundays

Murphy's Law

The War Within

Love's Bounty

Writing as Mason Dixon:

Date with Destiny

Charm City

LOVE'S BOUNTY

by
Yolanda Wallace

2015

LOVE'S BOUNTY
© 2015 By Yolanda Wallace. All Rights Reserved.

ISBN 13: 978-1-62639-334-9

This Trade Paperback Original Is Published By
Bold Strokes Books, Inc.
P.O. Box 249
Valley Falls, NY 12185

First Edition: April 2015

CREDITS
Editor: Cindy Cresap
Production Design: Susan Ramundo
Cover Design By Sheri (graphicartist2020@hotmail.com)

Acknowledgments

Deadliest Catch is must-see TV at my house. Every time Dita and I watch an episode, we wonder how an all-female crew would fare tackling the worst the Alaskan elements have to offer. *Love's Bounty* was inspired by those ruminations. I moved the setting from Alaska to Maine and changed from a hunt for crab to a search for lobster, but the battle against Mother Nature remains the same.

This book was a labor of love because it highlights one of my favorite parts of the country—the Northeast. I hope I have done justice to the region as well as the rugged individualists who call it home.

Thank you, once again, to Radclyffe and the women of BSB, who toil behind the scenes to make it look like I know what I'm doing. And thank you to the readers for making all the hard work so much fun.

Dedication

To Dita,
The best catch I ever made was landing you.

CHAPTER ONE

Shy Silva picked up her duffel bag from the dock and broke away from the line of people hoping to latch on to a job for the season. She should have known she wouldn't get the gig when she realized she was the only woman who had shown up today besides the captain. Then she had blown the interview by being honest instead of tactful. When the captain had asked her about her experience on the water, she should have lied and said she had plenty of it instead of admitting she'd never been on anything but a duck boat tour in her life. Not wanting to get off to the wrong start in what was supposed to be a new beginning, she had decided to be honest. And what would being honest get her? Exactly what she had expected all along: dismissed.

She stopped walking before she reached the end of the dock. She didn't want to be here begging for a job lobster fishing off the coast of Bumfuck, Maine, for the next seven months, but she didn't have a choice. If she didn't stand around eating humble pie with the rest of the bums with their hats in their hands, she wouldn't be eating anything for the foreseeable future.

Sending her to Portland had been her uncle Cristiano's idea. His way of protecting her from herself. He didn't approve of her friends—Lucy, especially—and didn't seem open to the idea of changing his mind.

"Just because you hang out with certain people doesn't mean you have to do the same things they do," he had said as he drove her to the bus station.

That was only the beginning of his lecture. She had tuned out the rest. She could have tried to defend herself, but he probably wouldn't have believed her anyway. Why should he? He had caught her telling too many lies—about where she'd been, who she'd been with, and how they'd spent their time—to think she would start being honest now.

"You can do better than what you're doing, Shy," Uncle Cristiano had said. "You can be better than the criminals you hang around with."

"They're not criminals," she had said defensively. "They're my friends."

"Try telling the cops that the next time they arrest you and your 'friends' for being drunk and disorderly outside that nightclub you love to frequent."

"My friends and I don't go looking for trouble. We're just trying to have a good time."

"You don't have to look for trouble. It has a way of finding you. How many times have you been arrested now, four or five?"

It was more like seven or eight, but Shy hadn't bothered to correct him.

"We're just bored and frustrated at being stuck in South Boston with nowhere to go and nothing to do. So we take drugs, get into fights, and commit the occasional petty crime for the thrill of getting away with it—or the notoriety of getting caught. No big deal."

"Bullshit," Uncle Cristiano had spat. "I grew up in this neighborhood, too. I went through the same things you did. But instead of taking the easy way out, I turned myself around. Now it's your turn. A summer in Portland will do you good. Working for Jake Myers will teach you the value of hard work."

Shy had chafed at her uncle's attempt to teach her a life lesson. She liked her life just fine. And if she wanted to learn the value of hard work, all she needed to do was watch her mother fight to make ends meet. Her mother had worked two and sometimes three jobs at a time since Shy's father died ten years ago. Her mother couldn't afford to buy Shy, her sister, or her two brothers everything they wanted, but she always made sure they had food to eat, clothes on their backs, and a place to lay their heads at night. Shy's family didn't have much, but they had each other.

"Maria has been carrying you, your sister, and your brothers on her back for years," Uncle Cristiano had said. "Now it's time for you to step up. Don't let me down, Shy. Don't let yourself down." In lieu of a hug, he had thrust several crumpled hundred dollar bills in her hand. "Now go show those Anglos what a Portuguese fisherman can do."

Reluctantly admitting to herself her uncle might be right about her and her friends—about almost everything, actually— Shy rejoined the three men lined up in front of the *Mary Margaret*, the boat she had been told to report to, and dropped her duffel between her feet. The dude closest to her looked like a meth head coming down from a high. His eyes were red, his hair looked like he had shampooed in an oil slick, and he smelled funkier than gourmet cheese. He sneered at her, flashing a mouthful of rotten or broken-off teeth.

"It's bad enough the captain of the boat's a chick. Now we've got to deal with female greenhorns, too?" He jerked a thumb in Shy's direction as he turned to his companions. "Someone should have told her she didn't need to pack every stitch of clothing she owns. Lobster fishing is a day trip."

Shy looked down at the duffel resting between the new pair of work boots she might not get to use. She knew the boat would go out in the morning and come back to shore in the afternoon, but she didn't have a place to stay yet and she didn't know what to do with her stuff in the meantime so she had brought it with her.

The guy to Yuckmouth's left, an older man who looked like he was in pain but was trying to hide it, took a quick glance in

Shy's direction. "Cut her a break, Charlie. She looks like she's in better shape than you or me."

Charlie's laugh had a hint of cruelty underneath the merriment. "Speak for yourself, old man. Ain't nothing a woman can do that a man can't do better."

"That's not what your girlfriend told me last night," Shy said under her breath.

Charlie whirled to face her, his hands balled into fists. "What did you say?"

"Nothing you haven't heard before," the young guy on the end said.

He looked to be around Shy's age. She was twenty-five. He was probably two or three years younger. With Anglos, it was hard to tell sometimes. With his perfect hair, crisp cotton shirt, and baggy cargo shorts, he looked like he had just stepped out of an Abercrombie and Fitch ad.

He had shown up after the interviews were over, either confident he would get the job or intentionally sabotaging his chances. Shy couldn't blame him if he was trying to avoid getting hired. Lobster fishing wasn't easy. Why would anyone volunteer to do it if they didn't have to? He probably didn't need this gig, anyway. A guy like him must have plenty of options. She, on the other hand, had only one: this one.

She had bombed out of every job she'd had, including working as a prep cook on Uncle Cristiano's food truck. With her track record, no one else in Southie would hire her. No one on the right side of the law, that was. She had plenty of chances to make money in ways that were less than legal, but she wasn't ready to go that way full-time. Yet.

"Mind your own business, college boy," Charlie said. "What are you doing here, anyway? I heard you were going to be working out of town this summer."

"Not that it's any business of yours, but yes, I plan to work in Orono while I take some extra classes. I came to tell Captain Jake before she heard it from anyone else."

"Too late. Good news travels fast," Charlie said, obviously thinking Pretty Boy's absence would improve his chances of making the small two- or three-person crew. "What's the matter? You too good for us now that you have a few years at the university under your belt?"

"Portland's my home," Pretty Boy said. "I'll never forget my hometown, though I'm not so sure I can say the same about some of the people in it."

He looked over and gave Shy a wink. She didn't know who he was, but she liked his style. He didn't take shit from anyone, but he used his head instead of his fists to defend himself. If she had tried to do that, her friends would have called her a coward. In her neighborhood, the only thing worse than being a coward was being a snitch. So she did what she had to do to make sure everyone around her knew she was neither. She fought when she should have walked away, and she kept her friends' secrets safe even when the burden of holding on to them was so much heavier than letting go.

As she waited for Captain Jake to let them know who she had decided to go with, Shy took in the various other boats moored to the dock. Lobster boats ranging in size from small wooden rowboats to forty-five-foot crafts with fiberglass hulls shared space with seventy-two-foot swordfish boats like the one in *The Perfect Storm*, a movie Shy had watched with one eye closed once the action shifted from the land to the ocean. She hoped the *Mary Margaret* would have better luck than the *Andrea Gail*. She shuddered as she remembered the scene where the boat tried to steer its way up the side of a massive wave only to fall short and go under, the crew members on board lost forever. She and Lucy had watched the movie because Mark Wahlberg, a fellow Southie, played one of the supporting roles. Watching his character bobbing in the water at the end with no hope of rescue made her never want to go near the ocean. Now she was trying to spend the next seven months making a living on it.

If she was lucky, maybe she could avoid dying in the process.

❖

Jacoby "Jake" Myers watched the testy exchange between Charlie, Tom, Zach, and the beautiful newcomer as she sat at the helm of the *Mary Margaret*. The cabin was small in comparison to the rest of the boat, leaving more room to store the hundreds of traps she and her crew tended to each day. She sprayed glass cleaner on the thick windshield designed to protect her from the elements as she piloted the boat. As she ran a paper towel over the reinforced glass, she thought about the hopefuls standing on the dock and tried to decide which one she should choose.

She normally went with a three-person crew. She manned the helm while Charlie and another crewman baited, set, and checked the traps. She always chose Charlie because he was her brother-in-law, but as his addiction worsened, more work fell on her and the other member of the crew. She was tired of propping him up, but she didn't have much choice. Tom's back was shot, Zach was taking the summer off, and the greenhorn Cristiano had sent her way didn't have any experience on the water. Charlie had experience, but he was notoriously unreliable. He was like that box of chocolates Forrest Gump kept going on and on about: she never knew what she was going to get. Should she go with the devil she knew or the one she didn't?

The decision of who to take and who to leave behind was exponentially more difficult this season, but giving herself more time to come to terms with her choice wasn't going to change the final outcome. She tugged on the bill of her baseball cap, pushed herself out of the worn leather seat she'd be occupying for the next seven months, and opened the cabin door.

The hopefuls stood at attention when they saw her standing on the deck. Tom visibly winced at the effort. Jake pretended not to notice as she stepped off the boat and onto the dock. Deciding to dispense with the pleasantries first, she extended her hand toward Zach.

"I'm sorry to hear you won't be joining us this year."

Zach looked anxious as he gripped her hand in his. "You heard."

"Portland's a small town. It didn't take me long to find out you were planning to leave me high and dry this year." Zach's face went pale and he tried to stammer an apology. Jake gave him a quick pat on the shoulder to let him know she didn't have any issues with the decision he had made. She hoped the others would feel the same way about hers. "I can't blame you for bailing, but what did you find to do in Orono that's better than smelling like bait all day?"

Zach grinned and let down his guard. "I got a job at the Fay Hyland Botanical Garden."

"Makes sense. You're majoring in botany, right?" Zach nodded. "Working at the botanical garden will be good experience for the future. Good luck in Orono. Maybe I'll see you the next time I get up that way." Jake hadn't ventured outside of the greater Portland area in nearly two years except for work, but Zach had the decency not to call attention to the promise they both knew she wouldn't keep. "Don't be a stranger, okay?"

"Thank you for the opportunity, Cap. I won't forget everything you and your family have done for me over the years."

"You can make it up by naming a flower after me."

He grinned again. "You don't strike me as a flower kind of girl. Cacti are pricklier. One of them would suit you better."

"Get out of here before I turn you into bait, smartass," she said with an easy laugh, something that had come at a premium over the past twenty-four months.

His hands shoved in the pockets of his voluminous shorts, Zach turned and walked away. Jake was going to miss the kid. Then again, he wasn't a kid anymore. He had come to her as an eighteen-year-old boy. Three years later, he was leaving a man. He had a bright future ahead of him, but he seemed destined for a life on land instead of the water.

Zach's best days were ahead of him. Jake's mood soured as she turned to a man who wasn't ready to accept the reality that his best days were behind him.

"How's the back holding up, Tom?"

Tom winced in real or remembered pain. "It's good. Real good," he said as he plastered on a smile that was a little too wide. Either the painkillers he popped like candy were wearing off or the ache from the ruptured discs in his back had grown too powerful to dull. "The wife bought a new brace that seems to be doing the trick. I should be good for two or three hours straight before I need to take a break."

Jake weighed her options. If Charlie proved to be as much of a screw-up this season as he normally was, most of the workload would fall on Tom. She doubted his iffy back, new brace or not, would hold up to the strain.

"I'm sorry, Tom, but I'm afraid I'm going to have to go in a different direction. Why don't you take the season off, give those discs some time to heal, and come see me next year?"

Tom tried and failed to hide his disappointment. His shoulders sagged along with his spirits.

"The wife has been nagging at me to break down and have surgery. We can afford it—we've got the money saved up for what the insurance won't cover—but I get stir crazy at the thought of being laid up for six weeks, and I've been too stubborn to admit I couldn't take the pain. It's getting to the point now where I can't play with my grandkids like they want me to. Like *I* want to." His chin started to tremble, and he bit his lip to keep from losing his composure. He cleared his throat, then shook his head as if he had come to a decision. "I've got to fix this. As soon as I get home, I'm going to call my doctor and make an appointment."

Jake wondered how long he would have kept trying to pretend everything was okay if he had found someone who was willing to take him on for the upcoming season. "See you next year?"

"You can count on it," he said before he walked away.

Charlie couldn't hide his glee after Tom's elimination left him and Cristiano's niece as the only ones in contention. He clapped his hands, as excited as his four-year-old son was whenever he discovered he was having pancakes for breakfast. "Looks like it's you, me, and the new girl this year, huh, Jake?"

"Actually, no, it isn't."

"What do you mean?"

"I've decided to go with a two-person crew this year."

"Cool. Splitting the profits two ways instead of three will give me a bigger cut at the end of the season. I can finally buy Jeannie and the kids some of the things they've been begging for."

The only person Jake thought would see any of the money Charlie got his hands on in the coming months was his dealer.

"Family first. Right, sis?" Charlie turned to Cristiano's niece. "Better luck next time. Why don't you go back to Massachusetts and try the Hooters in Saugus? A rack like yours would look pretty good in one of those tight white T-shirts. And your ass would look mighty tasty in a pair of those orange shorts."

"Fuck you, asshole."

Cristiano's niece—she had said her name was Ashley, but Jake suspected she went by something else—reached for her duffel. Trying not to smile at her willingness to put Charlie in his place, Jake held up a hand to stop her from leaving.

"Give us a minute." Ashley nodded and dropped her bag. Jake took a few steps away and beckoned for Charlie to follow. "Come here. I want to talk to you in private."

"About what?" He tried to look her in the eye, but his eyes wouldn't stop darting from side to side long enough to maintain contact with hers. He was in desperate need of a fix and it showed.

"I think you and I need to cut ties until you get clean."

"I am clean."

"Oh, yeah?" She put her hands on her hips to keep from shaking the truth out of him. "When was the last time you used?"

He lost a bit of defiance as he lowered his eyes in submission. "I might have had a little something last night to celebrate the start of the season, but I'll be right as rain when the season starts. I don't plan on partying again until December."

"Or until payday, you mean. I need someone I can count on."

"You can count on me."

"No, I can't. For years, I've been depending on the people around you to take up your slack. I'm done cutting you a break just because you're married to my sister. How can I be sure you won't get high at night and show up that way the next morning?"

"Because I told you I wouldn't. My word's still good for something, isn't it?"

"If I thought you could keep it."

She ignored the voice in her head that tried to convince her to go against her instincts and leave things as they were. Fishing, like life, was often more about luck than skill. She was as superstitious as anyone who fished for a living. Probably even more so. She depended on routine to keep her sane. To keep her safe. By breaking one of her established patterns, she might be putting herself and those she loved in danger. Again.

"I can't take the risk," she said, finding the courage to do what was right instead of what was easy. "Not when people's lives are on the line. I'm responsible for everyone on board my boat. That includes you and the people you let down when you show up at less than a hundred percent. I can't keep covering for you, Charlie. Neither can the rest of the crew. It's unfair to them, to me, and to you. What you need is some time to get everything out of your system. If you want to work while you do it, I hear Bruce Thornton is hiring. A few weeks at sea would do you good."

"Thorny's not a lobsterman," Charlie said contemptuously. "He hunts swordfish. Do you know how hard it is getting those things on deck? You're trying to hook them while they're trying to spear you. It's dangerous work."

"And this isn't?" Jake was offended by Charlie's implication that lobstering was easy, but she didn't want to pick a fight with him. The fight she was going to have with Jeannie after Charlie told her about her decision was going to be bad enough. "I don't have a place for you on my boat this year, Charlie. I'm sorry, but that's the way it is."

"I thought family was supposed to look out for family."

"That's what I've been doing for years. And that's exactly what I'm doing now."

"How? By taking food out of my kids' mouths?"

She had expected him to play the sympathy card, but if Jeannie couldn't force him to face his addictions, perhaps she could.

"I'm the one who's been putting food in your kids' mouths," Jake said, her voice rising. "Who do you think pays the bills when you can't? When you won't?"

She had lost track of the number of times Jeannie had asked her for handouts. Twenty bucks here. Fifty or a hundred there. But, knowing how badly Jeannie needed the money, Jake had given it away knowing she probably wouldn't get it back.

"I'll pay you back everything Jeannie and I owe you and then some," Charlie said, a promise as empty as the one she had made Zach a few minutes earlier. "If you want me to go work for Thorny, fine. You'll be doing me a favor. No one wants to work for you anyway. Why do you think only four people showed up today? Me, a broken-down old man, a wet-behind-the-ears newcomer who's never fished a day in her life, and a college boy who came just to tell you he was quitting."

Jake knew there was an element of truth to what Charlie was saying. An element she had been trying to ignore since the day everything had changed. Her personal life had been affected by the events of that day. Now the aftereffects were spreading to her professional life as well.

Her job wasn't as solitary as it appeared to be from the outside. As much as she might like to, fishermen didn't operate in vacuums. They relied on a vast network of social relationships for everything from the most productive fishing spots to the best market prices. She couldn't control what other people thought about her, but she had to stay in their good graces in order to make a living. If what Charlie said was true, she had her work cut out for her this season.

"We'll see what Jeannie and Kate have to say about what you've done." Charlie waved a dirt-encrusted finger in her face. "You're going to regret letting me go."

Jake hoped he was wrong. For both their sakes. After Charlie stalked away muttering curses and thinly-veiled threats under his breath, she took a moment to get a handle on her swirling emotions. Then she extended her hand. "Sorry you had to witness that, but it had to be done. Ashley, right?"

"That's right."

Ashley's voice was tentative, but her handshake was firm. Time would tell if she had the will to match.

"Ashley may be your given name, but I can tell you're not comfortable with it. We're going to be spending a significant amount of time together over the next seven months. What do you prefer to answer to?"

Ashley flashed a ghost of a smile. "My friends call me Shy."

Jake thought the name fit. Shy didn't say much, and when she did, Jake had to strain to hear her. Like Shy, her given name was something different, too, but she had been Jake ever since Jacoby Ellsbury started patrolling center field for the Red Sox. By the time he left the Sox to join the hated Yankees, it was too late to change back.

"Okay. Shy it is. Before we get started, I need you to tell me something."

"What?" Shy squared her shoulders as if preparing to defend herself against an attack. What did it mean that, when faced with a situation that made her uncomfortable, Shy's first inclination was to fight?

"Why are you here?"

"Why do you think? You've got a job opening and I want to work."

Jake didn't know which would prove to be the more difficult task, teaching Shy how to fish or breaking down her defenses.

"I'm sure you could have landed a job closer to home if you wanted to. Why did you come all the way to Portland to find work?"

Shy looked like she was searching for what to say, but she remained silent.

"Don't try to come up with what you think I want to hear," Jake said. "I don't want you to give me the 'right' answer. I want you to give me your honest answer. Are you here because your family sent you or because you want to be?"

"I'm here…because I've got nowhere else to go," Shy said hesitantly. "I'm here because I want to make something out of myself, and I think you can help me do it."

Shy's admission made Jake realize Shy had taken just as big a risk deciding to come to Portland as she had by asking her to stay. "Come aboard so I can show you around."

Shy picked up her duffel and slung it over her shoulder, but didn't make a move to follow her. "Now can I ask *you* something?"

"Sure. What do you want to know?"

"Why did you choose me?"

Jake had asked herself the same thing. When Cristiano had reached out to her cousin Kate, the boat's owner, he had asked her to give Shy a fair shake, but he hadn't asked her to give her a job. He had been made to earn his spot when he fished for Kate, and he wanted Shy to earn hers, too.

Shy had never been lobster fishing so she would do more learning than working in the beginning—if she recovered from the inevitable seasickness that struck all newcomers during their first few days on the job.

So why had Jake chosen her when she had more experienced potential crew members she could reach out to? Others who hadn't shown up today but might be available if the price was right.

Shy's Portuguese ancestry was evident in her slight accent, tawny skin, and wavy black hair. But Jake hadn't chosen her for her beauty. She had chosen her for something else. Something in the hazel eyes now looking questioningly into hers.

"I chose you because you remind me of me."

"How?" Shy asked, looking her up and down.

Jake felt an unexpected heat as Shy's eyes scoured her body. She knew they looked nothing alike—she was fair where Shy was dark and muscular where Shy was smooth—but she could tell they had something in common.

Some people said she was too young, too damaged, and too female to run her own boat. They said she had been given the captaincy of the *Mary Margaret* when Kate retired because she was family, not because she had earned the position on merit. The male hopefuls Jake had passed over today might say the same thing about Shy, but the chip on her shoulder Cristiano had mentioned made Jake think perhaps Shy had been judged prematurely as well. And that she would fight just as hard as Jake had to show she belonged.

"I chose you because we both have something to prove," Jake said. "Together, maybe we can do it. Are you with me?"

Her heart skittered in her chest as Shy looked her in the eye. "When do we start?"

CHAPTER TWO

S hy felt like she was being given a history lesson, but she made sure she was paying attention because listening to what Jake had to say could mean the difference between life and death. Hers.

"Maine is known for three things: Stephen King, lobster, and L. L. Bean," Jake said. "Not necessarily in that order."

The comment sounded pretty funny, but Shy wasn't sure if it was supposed to be a joke so she didn't laugh. It didn't matter anyway because Jake kept talking without waiting for a response. Her speech sounded rehearsed, and she sounded like she couldn't get through it fast enough so Shy wasn't about to stand in her way. The sooner they got the boring parts out of the way, the sooner they could get around to the exciting stuff. Like how much she was supposed to get paid.

"Maine produces more lobsters than any other state, and people have been fishing these waters for hundreds of years. Lobsters are plentiful now, but at one time, there were so many of them you could stand on the shore and catch them by hand. Nowadays, we use boats. Most boats have three-person crews, one to man the helm and two to haul the traps, also called pots. Even though we're a man short, I think we can get the job done. The work's hard, but it's rewarding, too."

Shy spoke up when Jake finally paused to take a breath. "Speaking of rewarding, how much will I get paid? We haven't discussed salary yet."

"I was coming to that."

Jake didn't sound irritated like her uncle Cristiano did whenever Shy interrupted one of his little speeches, but Shy could tell Jake didn't like having her rhythm disrupted when she was on a roll.

Note to self.

"The pay's twelve fifty an hour."

The figure was probably on the low end because she was a greenhorn, but to Shy, the number sounded astronomical. She had never made more than minimum wage for any job she had ever worked. And when she had worked for her uncle, he hadn't even paid her that much. The food was great, even if she made some of it herself, but the pay was lousy. She had been almost relieved when he'd fired her for being late more often than she was on time. She might have rejoiced at not having to try to live up to the strict standards he had set for himself and expected everyone else to meet if she hadn't been forced to deal with her mother's disappointment over her inability to hold down a steady job.

Things would be different this time, she vowed. They had to be.

"The typical work week is sixty hours, not counting offload time," Jake continued.

Her short-sleeved T-shirt showed off sinewy arms filled with lean muscle that attested to the many long hours she had put in steering the boat and manipulating the lobster traps. No wonder she hadn't been willing to take a chance on Tom and his bad back. Shy wondered if she'd have arms like that at the end of the season or if they took years instead of months to attain. She forced herself to pay attention to Jake's words instead of her body so she wouldn't start daydreaming about how it would feel to have those arms wrapped around her.

Jake was sneakily good-looking. You didn't notice how attractive she was when you first met her; it kind of crept up on you when you weren't paying attention. Her eyes were as blue as the ocean on which she made her living. And if the rest of her body was as ripped as her arms…Shy's mouth watered at the thought.

According to Uncle Cristiano, Jake was twenty-eight. She was only three years older than Shy, but she had everything Shy didn't. A good job, a place of her own, and the freedom to make her own decisions without being second-guessed all the time. Shy didn't have anything to offer a woman like that. A fling was out of the question, unless she wanted to risk losing the job she had barely won. And a relationship with someone of Jake's station was nothing more than a pipe dream. Shy decided it would be best if she kept her mind on business. She was supposed to be here to solve her problems, not cause more. Falling into bed with Jake Myers was one problem she didn't need, but it would certainly be a nice one to have.

"Some lobstermen work year-round, but the official season lasts from the first of May to the first week in December," Jake said. "For most of the season, no fishing can be done from half an hour before sunset until a half hour before sunrise. I typically work from five a.m. to five p.m. Monday through Friday. You'll get every weekend off and you'll get a break for lunch during the week, but we usually end up eating on the fly. Any questions so far?"

"No." With her brief fantasy safely stored in the back of her mind, Shy was too busy trying to wrap her head around the fact that she'd be pulling in seven hundred fifty dollars a week before Uncle Sam got his hands on it. Usually, she didn't see that much in a month.

"I'll cut you a check each week at the end of Friday's shift. When we're done here, I'll run you by the doctor's office so you can take a drug test and by the bank so you can open an account."

Shy hated pissing in a cup because she usually ended up with more urine on her hand than in the container, but she figured that wasn't a good enough excuse to get her out of the drug test so she didn't bother trotting it out. She didn't like the idea of her money being stuck where she couldn't get at it when she wanted it, though, so she said something about it.

"Can't you just pay me in cash?"

Jake looked at her as if she wondered what kind of under-the-table gigs Shy had worked in the past. If she didn't ask, Shy wasn't going to volunteer any answers.

"I could," Jake said carefully, "but the company accountant might not like me very much if I did. Have you found a place to stay yet?"

"I didn't know if I'd latch on so I didn't bother looking for a place with a vacancy." Her uncle had fronted her enough money to pay for her twenty-five-dollar train ticket from Boston to Portland on the Downeaster along with the first month's rent, but she'd need to find someplace cheap if she planned to eat more than once a day until she received her first paycheck. "I figure I'll check out the boardinghouses this afternoon."

Jake grimaced. "The season starts in a couple days. Chances are if you haven't booked a place by now, you're out of luck."

Shy felt stupid for downgrading her chances, but she had never gotten anything she really wanted and she hadn't expected today's outcome to be any different.

"What am I supposed to do now?"

Jake thought for a minute, her intense eyes scanning the horizon for answers. "Tell you what," she said at length. "My house used to be Kate's before it got too small to fit her and her family. A few years before I moved in, she turned the space above the garage into an apartment to accommodate crew members like you who were stuck without a place to stay. I could rent it to you for, say, seventy-five bucks a week. I could ask for more, but I'm not trying to gouge you. I'm just looking for enough income to cover the cost of the extra groceries and the increase in utilities. I could take the money out of your paycheck and you'd never feel a thing."

The deal sounded good. Too good.

"What's the catch?"

Jake took off her Portland Sea Dogs baseball cap and ran a hand through her light brown hair before she screwed the cap back into place. "I have trouble sleeping. I go to bed around eight during the week with the intention of getting up at four, but I usually wake up around one or two. Instead of tossing and turning and staring at the clock, I head to my woodshed and pull out my tools. I try to keep the noise down, but you might hear me banging around in the middle of the night."

Shy lived with her mother, sister, and two brothers in a cramped two-bedroom house. She was willing to endure listening to Jake pound a few nails at three in the morning in exchange for not waking up with a foot in her face, an elbow in her ribs, or a knee in the small of her back.

"It's a deal."

"Great. Now that that's settled, let me show you how the pots work."

Jake picked up a wire trap trimmed in thick plastic. Her broad hands were tanned and strong, the palms lightly callused.

"We'll set about five hundred of these on Thursday. We'll spend each day baiting them, checking on them, emptying them, rebaiting them, repairing them, and setting them again."

That explained the calluses.

"You put the bait here in this compartment in the front, which is called the chamber. The lobster gets trapped in the parlor in the back. We tie a marked buoy to each pot and drop the pots ten at a time. There's an escape vent on each pot so lobsters that don't meet the size requirements can pass through, and there's also a biodegradable ghost panel that allows a lobster trapped in a stranded pot to escape."

"How big do lobsters have to be to be considered keepers?"

Shy remembered the crews on *Deadliest Catch* keeping some of the crabs but throwing others back if they were too small. All of them looked good enough to eat, so she didn't understand the reasoning behind throwing perfectly good food overboard. That would be like trashing a pizza without taking a bite out of a single slice.

"Their carapaces have to be at least three and a quarter inches long or we toss them back. If we don't, we could get hit with a substantial fine."

Shy didn't know what a carapace was, but she was sure Jake would tell her when the time came. She'd lectured her on everything else today.

"We also toss back any egg-bearing females," Jake said, "but not before we notch a V in their tail fins to identify them."

"Doesn't cutting into their fins hurt them? When my friend Lucy got her belly button pierced, she said it hurt like a son of a bitch."

Jake almost laughed but fell just short. Her lips parted and curled into a smile, but no sound passed through them.

"I haven't heard any complaints yet." She gave Shy an inquisitive look. "I can see your eyes starting to glaze over, so we'll pick this up tomorrow. I'll show you where I keep the rain and survival gear and give you a tour of the helm. After we get all our errands run, we'll grab something to eat and get you settled in the apartment. Make sure you get plenty of rest tonight. Tomorrow's going to be a long day."

Shy suspected the ones that followed would be just as bad.

❖

Jake began to second-guess herself even before she backed her truck out of the parking lot. When she checked her cell phone, she had four missed calls and three voicemails from Jeannie, each angrier and more desperate than the last.

Jeannie was older by two years, yet Jake had always assumed the role of protective big sister, shielding Jeannie from everything from schoolyard bullies to overly-amorous boyfriends who didn't know how to take no for an answer. Jake had thought she was doing the right thing all these years, but perhaps she was wrong. Perhaps allowing Jeannie to receive a few more bumps and scrapes as she made her way through life would have helped her avoid the mess she was in now, married to a man who couldn't provide for the three kids they already had, let alone the one on the way.

She put her phone away and focused on the road while she made the short fifteen-minute trip from the docks to town. As she slowed for one of Portland's many retirees taking his antique car out for a thirty-mile-per-hour spin, she hazarded a glance at her new hire.

Instead of taking in the awesome beauty of Maine's rocky coastline or the architectural wonders of the historic buildings lining the streets of Old Port, Shy was focused on the texts she was sending and receiving on her phone. Every few seconds, her fingers would dance across the on-screen keyboard and her eyes would sparkle with delight after she read the responses to what she had written.

Jake felt a pang of jealousy as unexpected as the arousal she had experienced on the dock earlier when Shy eyed her from head to toe. She mentally chided herself. She had never slept with any of her previous crew members—it helped that they had all been male—and she wasn't about to start now.

After the driver of the eighty-year-old roadster turned off the highway with a high-pitched toot of his horn and a friendly wave to the long string of cars trailing behind him, Jake broke the growing silence.

"Your uncle says you're the oldest of four."

"Yeah, my brother Danny's eighteen, my sister Laura's fifteen, and my little brother Federico is about to turn twelve."

"As the oldest, you must be used to being responsible."

Shy looked at her as if Jake had accused her of being the opposite. "I do what I can to help out. Family's important to me."

"That's what your uncle says. He speaks highly of you."

Shy looked at her distrustfully, then shoved her phone in the pocket of her windbreaker. "I find that hard to believe," she said as she turned to stare out the window.

"I assure you he had nothing but nice things to say about you."

"He should try saying them to my face sometime."

There it was. The bad attitude Cristiano had warned Kate about. Jake hoped Shy would let her help identify the source of her anger rather than take it out on everyone around her. Jake was hard enough on herself. She didn't need anyone else piling on.

"What do you do back in Boston? Do you have someone eagerly waiting to hear about all the adventures you're going to have this season?"

Shy turned to face her. "Do you always ask this many questions?"

Jake nearly laughed out loud at the unintended absurdity of the question. "Don't get used to it. Once the fishing starts and we find our rhythm, you might not get more than two words out of me all day."

Jake half-expected Shy to say she couldn't wait for the mind-numbing, backbreaking work to begin. Instead, she was quiet for a long moment before she hesitantly asked, "So what did Uncle Cristiano say about me?"

Jake turned away to hide her smile. "He said you were smart and hardworking and all you needed was a chance to get out of your own way."

"Get out from underfoot, you mean." Shy picked at the truck's faux leather upholstery with her fingernail, betraying the uncertainty and hunger for approval that seemed to lie just beneath her surface.

"Is there something you wanted to ask me?" Jake said.

"Yeah. As a matter of fact, there is."

Shy's eyes looked disconcertingly serious. Jake braced herself for a question she might not be ready to answer. The first one or the others that would surely follow.

"Is it true what that guy said about you?"

"Who? Charlie?" Jake's stomach tightened after Shy nodded. She looked away to hide her anxiety. "He said a lot of things. Which one in particular are you referring to?"

"The part about no one wanting to work for you. Is it true? If it is, is it because you're a chick or what? I mean, fishing's a man's game, right?"

"For the most part."

"What makes you think you can change that?"

"You mean *we*, don't you? You're a part of this now, too."

"What if I'm not ready to take on the challenge?"

"Do you feel like you're ready?"

Shy hesitated the same way she had when Jake had asked her if she had any experience on the water.

"I've never done anything like this before, but if you think I'm up to the challenge, maybe I am."

"I wouldn't have selected you if I didn't believe in you."

Shy didn't say anything in response, but her eyes lit up at the compliment. Their arrival at Dr. Halloran's office brought the conversation to an unsatisfying end. Jake found a parking spot out front and switched off the engine.

"Let's go inside so we can get you taken care of."

She climbed out of the truck and slammed the door behind her, wondering if Shy thought she was a soft touch, a hard-ass, a head case, or all three. Today, it felt like a toss-up.

❖

After they left the doctor's office, Shy followed Jake up the sidewalk and through the double doors of Old Port National Bank. She wished she could take back what she'd said in the truck—Jake's demeanor had changed as soon as she asked about the comment Charlie had made—but she wanted to know what she was getting into.

She thought it was pretty badass for a woman to try to make a living in a male-dominated field. She probably should have led with that instead of reminding Jake of all the hurtful things Charlie had said to her when she told him she had decided not to hire him.

Mama always says I speak before I think. Maybe she's right.

Inside the bank, Jake approached the Accounts desk and greeted a middle-aged woman whose bottle-blond hair had been teased and sprayed into a style that was at least thirty years out of date. "Hey, Rita. How are you doing today?"

"I can't complain, Jake. And if I did, I doubt anyone would listen."

"You got that right. This is Shy. She's going to be working for me this season so she needs to open an account."

Shy moved closer after Jake waved her over to the desk.

"Shy, huh?" Rita looked over the tops of her half-moon-shaped reading glasses. "You're just as bashful as your name. Have a seat. I promise I won't bite too hard." After Shy settled into one of the two chairs in front of the desk, Rita said, "Now give me two forms of ID so we can get started."

Shy fished her driver's license and Social Security card out of her wallet.

"What kind of account were you hoping to open today?" Rita asked as she discreetly compared the photo on the license to Shy's face.

"A checking account, I guess."

"Then today's your lucky day," Rita said with a friendly smile, "because we happen to offer several of those. Let me run a quick credit check and we'll see which ones you qualify for."

Shy didn't like the sound of that. She didn't have bad credit. More like no credit at all. She had never had a credit card or a checking account or bought anything that cost more than what she had on her at the time. None of the credit bureaus probably knew she existed. Sure enough, Rita's smile faded into a frown as soon as the credit report popped up on her computer screen.

"Hmm," Rita said, clicking through screens on her monitor. "You don't seem to have much of a credit history."

Her cheeks flushed with embarrassment, Shy reached for her ID cards and stood to leave. "I told Jake this was a mistake. I'm sorry to have wasted your time."

"Hold on. Not so fast." Rita waved Shy back into her seat. "We have a special checking account for potential customers who might not qualify for a product with all the bells and whistles. You wouldn't be issued a debit card, but you could have access to all the other standard features—a free set of starter checks, the ability to sign up for online banking, federal insurance on balances up to two hundred fifty thousand dollars, and, last but not least, the best customer service in all of New England." She slid a thick three-ring binder across the desk. "Here are the latest designs our check vendor offers. If you can answer a few basic questions while you pick a pattern you like, we'll be done in no time."

Shy didn't know what to say as she flipped through the notebook's laminated pages. The people in this town were strangers, yet most of the ones she had encountered had gone out of their way to help her. Just like with the offer Jake had made to rent her an apartment for next to nothing, she kept looking for the catch.

"You *are* a shy one, aren't you?" Rita asked with an amused shake of her head. "I know one thing. The *Mary Margaret* will be one quiet boat with you and Jake working side-by-side."

Shy looked over at Jake, who was chatting with one of the tellers. The teller's obvious ease at being in Jake's presence seemed at odds with Charlie's statement about the whole town being against her. Shy didn't know who or what to believe. She was an outsider here. She couldn't count on anyone to tell her the truth.

"How long have you known Jake?" Shy asked.

"She and my daughter, Susan, were as thick as thieves growing up," Rita said, not taking her eyes off the screen as she input information into the electronic form displayed on the monitor. "Jake was at my house so much back then she was practically part of the family. She still feels like one, even though she doesn't come over nearly as often. I always thought she and Susan would—" She caught herself. "Well, it doesn't matter what I thought."

"Do you like her?"

"Jake?" Rita's eyes flicked up and settled on hers. "Honey, they don't come any better. You know how they say some people would give you the shirts off their backs? If you needed them, Jake would give you her coat, pants, socks, and shoes, too."

The comment made Shy imagine Jake wearing nothing but her underwear, which was a surprisingly pleasant thought. The way Jake's jeans hugged her ass as she leaned in the teller's window made Shy want to see if the curves were real or an optical illusion.

"Why do you ask?" Rita's question pulled Shy out of her reverie. "Has someone been talking about her behind her back?" Rita's eyebrows knitted in barely-suppressed rage as her protective maternal instincts came to the fore. "If so, tell me who and I'll be sure to set them straight."

Shy wasn't looking to get involved in someone else's beef. "No one said anything. I was just curious."

Other people's opinions of Jake didn't matter, anyway. She needed to form her own.

"All set?" Jake asked as Shy clutched the documents Rita had given her to keep. "If you are, I have a pile of paperwork for you to sign that's going to make the stuff in your hand pale in comparison."

"I thought we were going to get something to eat." Nervous energy had made Shy burn through the little bit of food she'd had for breakfast, and she'd been too busy trying to find the dock to stop for lunch.

"We can do that," Jake said. "I'll buy you a cup of lobster chowder at the Watering Hole while you sign your life away. It's about time you got a taste of what you're going to be fishing for."

Chapter Three

The Watering Hole was "only" seventy-five years old so it hadn't been around nearly as long as some of the other buildings in town, but it was just as much of a fixture in Old Port as the centuries-old edifices that surrounded it.

Kate's wife, Tess, used to be a barmaid at the Watering Hole, but after a push—along with a substantial investment—from Kate, she had bought the business when the previous owner decided to sell out. Despite her new title, however, Tess's favorite place was still behind the bar, which was where Jake spotted her when she and Shy walked in.

"Afternoon, Jake. Who's your friend?" Tess asked as she prepared drinks for a pair of out-of-towners.

Jake took a seat at the bar. "This is Shy. She'll be working the boat with me this season. Shy, Tess Myers. Tess is our boss's wife, so be careful what you say about the company in front of her."

Tess served the freshly made drinks and wiped down the bar top with a towel. "Kate's got her business and I've got mine. Talk about both ends as soon as we leave our respective offices."

"Kate's 'office' is pretty sweet," Jake said for Shy's benefit. "Since she gave up fishing, she runs the company from her house, usually perched in her La-Z-Boy with a drink in one hand and the TV remote in the other."

"I wish I had a job like that," Shy said.

"Stick around long enough and you just might," Tess said. She pulled a bottle of Allagash White, a Belgian-style wheat beer, from the cooler, popped the top, stuck an orange slice on the side, and placed the bottle in front of Jake. The brand was Jake's favorite of all the brews the bar served, partly because of its local ties. "What'll you have, Shy?"

"I'll try one of those."

Tess grabbed another Allagash, along with a menu. She placed both within Shy's easy reach. "How long have you been fishing?"

"I'm just getting started. Tomorrow will be my first day."

"You'll be fine. Jake runs a tight ship, but you could learn a lot from her."

Shy took a tentative sip of her beer, evidently found it worthy of a longer swallow, and focused on the menu. Her eyes darted across the various selections. "So I've heard."

"Where's Kate?" Jake asked, giving Shy some time to decide what she wanted to order.

"She took Morgan by the sporting goods store to pick up a pair of cleats. He's outgrown the ones from last year, and he wants to get plenty of practice in this summer so he can make junior varsity in the fall."

"How's his fastball coming?"

"It's even better than his brother's was at the same age, but Pete's curve still has Morgan's beat by a mile," Tess said with no small measure of pride. She had reason to brag. Pete was a starting pitcher for the Portland Sea Dogs, and scouts said he was one of the Red Sox's top prospects. Morgan was determined to follow in his big brother's footsteps. All the way to the major leagues. "Pete has a game this weekend. You coming out to see him? Binghamton's in town. The teams are playing for first."

Tess extended an invitation every time Pete was scheduled to pitch a home game. She knew what Jake's answer would be even before she asked the question, but she kept asking nevertheless.

Jake admired her persistence. It tore at her heart to say no, but she didn't have the strength to say yes. Not yet.

"I'll try and catch the broadcast on the radio."

"It's been two years, Jake," Tess said softly. "When are you going to move on?"

"When I'm ready."

Jake took a long draw of her beer. She wished she could swallow her pain as easily as she did the lager. She had stopped living the day she cheated death. Scores of people had told her to put the experience behind her, but no one had been able to tell her how.

She turned to listen to the late afternoon entertainment, a singer performing lovelorn ballads featuring men drawn to the sea and women praying for their safe return.

"Is Kate planning on coming by here when she and Morgan are done shopping?" she asked during the break between sets.

"She'll be by in a few," Tess said. "I'm guessing Jeannie will be, too. She's already dropped in twice looking for you, loaded for bear both times."

"Yeah, I wanted to talk to Kate about that."

"There's nothing to talk about."

Jake turned at the sound of her cousin's familiar alto. Kate had fished for thirty of her fifty years. She had started apprenticing on her father's boat when she was eighteen and became captain of her own when she was twenty-two. A few years after she and Tess got together, she had decided to retire early in order to spend more time with Tess and the boys. Jake had taken over the boat, but the business was still Kate's. That was fine by Jake. She didn't have the temperament to deal with all the behind-the-scenes stuff. She would rather pilot a boat during a nor'easter than stress over spreadsheets and flow charts.

"I trust your judgment, Jake," Kate said. "I'm sure Ashley will work out real well for us."

"Hi, Cousin Jake," Morgan said.

"Hey, little man," Jake said, giving him a high five.

Morgan had his mother's kelly green eyes and flaming red hair. He and his brother both. Like Pete, Morgan had inherited his father's height but, thankfully, not his fondness for domestic violence. Owen Moody's mistreatment of Tess had been the talk of the town for years. Each time Tess showed up to work with a black eye, men and women alike had whispered what they would do to Owen if they could get their hands on him, but only Kate had had the balls to get off her barstool and do something about it.

"Is this your new crew mate?" Morgan asked.

"Sure is. This is Shy."

"Hello, Shy. I'm Morgan." He stuck out his hand for a shake.

"Nice to meet you, Morgan."

"You're cute."

Shy cocked her head. "What are you, thirteen? Aren't you too young to be ogling girls?"

Morgan grinned. "Mama Kate said I got an early start."

"He was born premature and has been ahead of the game ever since." Kate held out her hand, too. "Good to meet you, Shy. If you're half the lobster magnet your uncle was, you and Jake will fill the *Mary Margaret's* hold in no time at all."

"I'll do my best."

"I'm sure you will." Kate turned to Tess as the relief bartender arrived. "Ready to go, babe?"

"Let me put Jake and Shy's food order in first. Then we can head home. What'll it be, you two?"

"I'll have my usual," Jake said. "Start Shy off with a cup of lobster chowder and throw in whatever else she wants. I'm buying."

"All right then." Tess scribbled something on her order pad and turned to Shy. "Have you found something that tickles your fancy?"

Shy closed the menu. "I'll have a grilled chicken sandwich with a side of sweet potato fries."

Tess chuckled. "You two are a matched set, aren't you?"

Shy looked like she thought she was the butt of a joke she didn't understand. "What do you mean?"

"You'll see." Tess entered the orders in the computer and hit Enter to send them to the kitchen. "Enjoy your meal and, more importantly, have a safe season," she said before she gathered her things and left with her family in tow.

Jake picked up her beer. "Let's grab a booth. You can fill out these forms while we wait for our food to arrive."

"What kind of forms are they?"

Jake opened the folder she'd brought inside with her and slid it toward Shy, along with a pen she pulled out of her shirt pocket. "Insurance applications, payroll tax forms. The usual stuff. Didn't you have to complete something similar when you worked in your uncle's food truck?"

"No. I didn't work for him long, and he wasn't nearly as strict about these things as you are."

"When you run your own business, you can play by your own rules. When you work for someone else, you have to follow the rules that are laid out for you."

"Do you want to run your own boat one day?" Shy asked as she began to complete the forms.

"No, I'd rather make them."

"Is that what you do in your woodshed at night when you can't sleep?"

"You remembered that, did you?" Jake leaned forward in her seat and watched the bar begin to fill. Taking a deep breath, she fought the urge to escape. "Boat building is a hobby of mine. I fish from May to December so I can build boats the rest of the time."

"Are you working on one now?"

"Always."

"Is it for a client?"

"The ones I work on from January through April are for other people. This one's for me." Jake felt the tense muscles in her shoulders begin to relax. Talking to Shy helped relieve her growing anxiety. "Do you have any hobbies?" she asked.

Shy shrugged. "Not really. I just like to hang out with my friends. Sometimes Lucy and I talk about going to Fenway to watch the Sox play, especially when the Yankees are in town, but we can never get the hookup on tickets. They're either sold out or the price is too high."

"You like the Sox?"

"Who doesn't?" Shy finally displayed some enthusiasm. She became fully engaged as she listed her favorite players past and present. "Ted Williams. Carl Yastrzemski. Nomar Garciaparra. Dustin Pedroia. And don't forget Big Papi. Whether they're winning or losing, that's my team. Lucy's more of a fair-weather fan. If the Sox lose a few games in a row, she jumps off the bandwagon. When they have a winning streak, she jumps right back on. Me? I'm there all the time, whether we're winning the World Series or finishing last in our division."

"Who's Lucy?"

"The main reason I'm stuck here for—" Shy caught herself. "I mean, she's just a friend." She slid the completed forms across the table. "Here are your papers. Are we done now?"

"Yeah," Jake said, already missing the spark she had briefly seen in Shy's eyes. The unbridled joy she had seen on her face. "We're done."

❖

The waiter brought out their appetizers, a house salad for Jake and lobster chowder for Shy. Shy stirred the steaming stew and gave it time to cool. Lobster was outside her family's budget so she'd never had any before. She hoped it wasn't one of those things people went on and on about but, despite its great reputation, actually tasted like ass.

She hesitantly brought the spoon to her mouth and took a bite. The combination of roasted corn, savory potatoes, sweet lobster meat, and rich cream was so good she reached the bottom of the bowl much too soon. She had to resist picking up the empty cup and licking it clean.

"Want another one?" Jake asked, barely suppressing a smile.

Shy pushed the cup away from her so a roving waiter or busboy could clear it from the table. "Nah, I'm good."

She looked around the room. The place wasn't full yet, but more and more people were drifting in every minute. Most seemed to know each other, but the people in this town were so friendly it was hard to tell.

The Watering Hole had a nautical theme. Not surprising since it was located in a fishing town. A plaque over the front door read, "Welcome to the Watering Hole. Where Sea Dogs Come to Rest Their Paws." An old carving of a female figure that could be or might have been a masthead of a ship hung over the bar. One wall was covered with photographs of professional and amateur fishermen showing off their prize catches. Shy still couldn't believe she had a chance to join their ranks. Despite her own doubts about her ability to get the job, she had made the cut. Now she had to make sure she didn't get chopped.

Nothing about this day—or this town—felt real. She wanted to talk to someone about it. Once Jake stopped dragging her all over town, maybe she'd have a chance to give Lucy a call—and tell her mother she wouldn't be catching a ride home on the next train.

Jake polished off her salad just in time for the waiter to bring their entrees. Shy did a double take when she realized she and Jake had ordered the same thing. Jake's "usual" was what had appealed to her, too: a grilled chicken sandwich with a side of sweet potato fries.

"Was this what Tess meant when she said we were a matched set?"

"Ayuh," Jake said as she squirted ketchup on her fries. "It is."

When she had first laid eyes on the hard-nosed Anglo who was now her new boss, Shy hadn't thought they had anything in common except a fondness for baseball. Now she wondered what other interests they might share.

"Is this your lucky meal or something?" she asked. "Is that why you have it all the time?"

"You could say that," Jake said between bites of her sandwich.

Jake didn't seem willing to elaborate and Shy didn't feel like dragging anything out of her so they ate in silence. Shy didn't mind. The quiet was kind of nice. Comfortable even. Shy didn't feel rushed or hurried or, more importantly, judged.

She was beginning to like it here.

CHAPTER FOUR

When Jake pulled up to her house, a two-story Victorian with a detached garage, Jeannie was sitting on the front steps, her growing baby bump visible even from thirty feet away.

"I knew you had to come home sometime." Jeannie pushed herself to her feet as Jake and Shy spilled out of the truck. "Is this your girlfriend, the one you gave Charlie's job to?"

"Shy isn't my girlfriend, and yes, she's my employee." Jake tossed Shy the keys to the apartment over the garage. "Why don't you head upstairs? I'll be up in a few to make sure you have everything you need."

"Okay." Shy tossed her duffel over her shoulder and headed toward the garage.

"Moving her in and everything," Jeannie said bitterly. "I guess you're planning on having her stick around a while."

Jake took Jeannie by the arm. "Let's go inside so we can talk."

Jeannie freed her arm with a jerk. "What's the matter? Don't you want your girlfriend to hear what I have to say about you?"

Shy looked back as if to make sure everything was okay, then continued walking toward the stairs that led to the apartment over the garage.

Jake unlocked her front door and let Jeannie go in first. "Where are the kids?"

"Ma said she'd look after them for a while."

Jeannie sank heavily onto the sofa and rubbed her rounded belly. Each pregnancy seemed to take more out of her. Jake wondered how Jeannie and Charlie would survive the coming months if he didn't latch on with Bruce Thornton's crew. She doubted anyone would hire Jeannie knowing she would work for only three or four months max before she'd be putting in for six weeks of maternity leave.

"Would you like something to drink?" Jake asked.

"I'd love a shot of tequila, but I can't have one until this one's out and weaned off my tit." Jeannie's gray eyes narrowed. "Don't change the subject. You know why I'm here. Why did you pass Charlie over?"

Jake sat across from her. "Don't pretend you don't know."

"I know he's got his problems."

"And his problems are getting worse."

"You can't prove that. He's passed every piss test you've ever given him."

"I always suspected he found a way to sneak a sample of someone else's urine into the testing facility. Maybe yours or one of the kids'."

"He couldn't use mine unless he wanted to explain why he failed the pregnancy test," Jeannie said with a snort of laughter, but her laughter quickly faded before Jake could think about joining in. "We're hurting, Jake. Charlie needs this job. Don't make me beg you for it."

Jake felt her resolve begin to erode but forced herself to stand firm. "I want to help, but he's got to help himself first."

Tears filled Jeannie's eyes. "So what are we supposed to do, mooch off of Ma and Pop?"

"I don't know, Jeannie, but I'm sure you'll think of something."

Jeannie scowled. "You're one hard bitch, you know that? No wonder Susan doesn't want anything to do with you anymore."

Jake flinched as Jeannie's barb hit its mark. "That's not fair. Leaving Portland was her idea, not mine."

"But going to Boston that day was yours, wasn't it?"

"And I've been regretting it ever since. But that day has nothing to do with why we're sitting here now. If Charlie gets clean, he might be able to work for me next season. Until then, I wish you the best of luck."

"Love you, too, little sister," Jeannie said as she marched toward the door. "I hope you and your girlfriend can handle it by yourselves. Otherwise, you're going to be the laughingstock of the whole fleet."

"We'll manage," Jake said to Jeannie's departing back. "I always do."

"When are you going to realize that not everything's about you?"

Jeannie slammed the door before Jake could remind her she had already learned that particular lesson all too well.

❖

Shy watched through the apartment window as the pregnant woman—Jake's sister, she was guessing—climbed into a beat-up Saturn and burned rubber down the street.

"She's leaving," she said into the phone.

"And she's probably taking your job with her," Lucy said.

"I doubt it. She looks too pissed off to have gotten her way."

"You don't *want* to stay up there, do you?"

"If I came home now, Uncle Cristiano would think I'm a failure."

"He thinks that anyway."

The comment stung more than it usually did.

"Thanks, Luce. You're the best friend a girl ever had."

"Aw, you know I didn't mean nothing by it. I just can't believe you'd rather be up there in the middle of nowhere than here in Southie where all the action is. Hector's having a rent party Friday night. It's a shame you're going to miss it. We could have had some fun."

Shy thought about the last party Hector had thrown. She and Lucy had smoked a bag of weed and made love all night. The next day, Lucy had asked her not to tell anyone what had happened between them because she wasn't gay; she was just doing her thing.

Shy had reluctantly agreed because her attraction to Lucy was as powerful as the weed they had smoked that night and she wanted another hit.

"Do you really have your own apartment?" Lucy asked. "It must be kind of nice not to have to share space for a change."

"Yeah, it is pretty sweet."

The apartment wasn't fancy, but it had everything she could possibly want: her own TV, bedroom, and bathroom. Even a living room and a little kitchen where she could cook her own meals if she felt like it. The wide windows looked out on a neighborhood that was nothing like the one she was used to. Despite everyone's best efforts to make her feel welcome, she didn't feel like she belonged here. She wondered if the feeling would ever go away.

"Maybe I could come up and see you sometime," Lucy said. "Give you a little taste of home. Would you like that?"

"You know I would."

"If I can scrape some money together for a train ticket, I might surprise you some weekend."

"Cool. You can't bring any weed, though."

"Why not? I thought you liked to party with me."

"I do, but Jake fired Charlie for taking drugs and he was her brother-in-law. What do you think she'd do to me?"

"Fine. No weed. I'll have to find something else to get you going."

"I need to get blunted to relax in front of a crowd, but when we're alone, all I need is you, Luce."

"Does your boss know you're gay?"

"Not unless Uncle Cristiano told her. She and I haven't talked about our personal lives."

"Good. Keep it that way. No one needs to know your business but you. I've got to go, beautiful. Text me the address so I'll know where to find you."

"Sure thing."

"Don't swallow too much salt water, all right?"

"I'll try not to."

Shy ended the call, feeling more settled than she'd felt all day. She had a job, a nice place to stay, and something to look forward to. When Jake knocked on the door to ask if there was anything she needed, she couldn't think of anything to add. What more could she possibly want?

"Make sure you get plenty of sleep," Jake said. "We've got a full day tomorrow. We need to inspect all the traps and make sure the off-season repairs I made when the boat was in dry dock will hold up to the rigors of the season. We'll have some breakfast and head to the dock around eight."

"I'll be ready," Shy said, making a mental note to set the alarm on her phone to wake her in plenty of time. Jake turned to leave, but Shy wasn't ready to see her go. Not after the scene she'd witnessed through the window. She hadn't heard most of it, but Jake's body language had told her all she needed to know. Jake was sticking by her decision to hire her, even if it ended up affecting her relationship with her family. Shy didn't know how to help make things better, but she wanted to give it a try. "Are you okay?"

"What do you mean?" Jake looked at her with guarded eyes.

"The way that lady took off, I thought something might be wrong."

Jake's gaze softened and some of the hard edge went out of her voice. "Don't worry about it, okay? Just do the job I hired you to do and everything will work out. I'll see you in the morning."

As Jake jogged down the stairs, Shy felt the pressure to succeed ratchet up even higher. She had to make this work. Not just for her sake. For Jake's, too.

She called her mother, craving the sound of her voice and the soothing effect it always had on her.

"Hello?"

Her mother sounded tired. Since it was a weekday, she had worked eight hours as a maid at a luxury hotel in downtown Boston and had probably come home just long enough to grab something to eat and take a quick nap before she headed off to her job as a waitress at a local all-night diner. On the weekends, she worked part-time at the neighborhood *bodega*.

Shy wished her mother could work one job instead of three, but her mother couldn't afford to slow down. The family needed every penny of her meager salaries. Now, perhaps, Shy could help her out instead of bringing her down.

"I got the job," Shy said.

"Really?"

Her mother's voice was filled with a mixture of pride and surprise. Shy felt the same way. She was proud Jake had chosen her but surprised her new boss hadn't selected someone who had more experience.

"I knew you could do it, Shy."

"Did you?"

"No," her mother admitted with a weary laugh, "but I prayed about it."

Prayer was her mother's go-to response for everything. Shy preferred to handle her problems herself instead of turning them over to someone else, but, for the moment, she'd take all the help she could get.

"Tell me everything," her mother said.

Shy told her about her missteps during the interview, her confrontation with Jake's brother-in-law while they waited to see who Jake had chosen to be her mate, her trip to the Watering Hole after the big announcement, and her impressions of her new apartment. She saved the best news for last.

"Based on the salary Jake quoted me, I'm going to be making enough money to send some home. I'll mail you a check every week after I get paid."

"Save your money, Shy. Buy yourself something nice. Buy yourself the things I could never get you."

Most of Shy's other paychecks—while they lasted—had gone toward purchasing high-tech toys, Timberland boots, and designer jeans. All the things Shy had wanted when she was a teenager but her mother couldn't afford. Things that had meant the world to Shy at the time but didn't seem to matter much now.

"That's okay, Mama. I want to help."

"I could use the assistance," her mother said with a grateful sigh. "Federico's growing like a weed. I think he's gone through three sizes in the past month."

Her mother's words were muffled as she unsuccessfully tried to stifle a yawn.

"Get some sleep, Mama," Shy said softly. "I'll call you tomorrow, okay?"

"Take care, Ashley. And don't stress too much about being away from home. If you stay in your place, be respectful, and remember everything your father and I taught you, everything will be fine."

Shy would rather forget some of the lessons her father had imparted before he died, but this wasn't the time to bring it up.

"Good night, Mama."

"Good night, baby. Make me proud."

"I'll try."

Shy went to bed around nine but couldn't fall asleep. She wasn't used to having something to lose. Fear and dread kept her awake as she tossed from one side of the bed to the other.

The neighborhood was too quiet. She missed the lullaby of home. The comforting sound of her sister's breathing. The clamor of cars passing on the street and neighbors arguing in the house next door.

She had never felt more alone.

She gripped the spare pillow tight to keep from coming apart. She needed someone to hold. Someone to chase away her doubts and tell her she wasn't going to wash out. She closed her eyes and tried to convince herself.

When she finally dozed off, the sound of muffled banging jerked her awake. She picked up her phone to check the time. The display read three a.m., four hours before her alarm was scheduled to chime.

She padded to the side window and looked out. A sliver of light peeked from beneath the shed door. After she raised the window, she heard hammering and sawing from inside the shed. Jake was working on her boat.

Shy leaned her arms on the windowsill. She wanted to go downstairs and take a closer look, but Jake hadn't invited her inside her private domain and Shy didn't want to intrude. So she lowered the window and climbed back in bed.

As the muffled sounds continued, she tried to imagine what kind of boat Jake was building. Something simple to keep her mind occupied or something more elaborate to show off her skills?

Shy felt envious in a way. She didn't know what it was like to have something that was hers and no one else's. Maybe one day she'd find out.

CHAPTER FIVE

Jake backed her truck up to the storage unit and jumped out to lower the gate on the attached trailer.

"We have to load all five hundred of them today?" Shy asked as she peered at the traps neatly stacked inside the unit.

She sounded exhausted and they hadn't even gotten started. The work could be mind-numbing if you thought about it too long. Usually, Jake relied on muscle memory and let her mind drift to thoughts of something more pleasant.

"We have to load them in the truck and transfer them to the dock after we make sure none of them need repairing or replacing. Tomorrow, we'll take them out, bait them up, tie a buoy to each one, toss them over the side, then cross our fingers and pray they end up filled with keepers." She pulled a pair of work gloves out of her back pocket. "There's an extra pair of these in the glove compartment. Why don't you try them on and see if they fit? The wire in the traps hurts like a mother when it slices into your skin, but the tetanus shot you'd have to get hurts even worse."

Shy reached into the truck and pulled on the gloves. Her hands were about the same size as Jake's, but she was taller so her fingers were slightly longer. Delicate and tapered like a musician's.

"How do they feel?" Jake asked as Shy flexed her hands in the worn leather gloves to test the feel.

"Perfect fit."

Jake showed her how to inspect the traps to see if any wires were broken and taught her how to repair them if they were. Shy caught on quickly. She turned to Jake for guidance a time or two, then began to trust her own instincts. Gradually, the pile of traps on the trailer began to dwarf the pile in the storage unit rather than vice versa.

"That didn't take as long as I thought," Shy said after the last trap was secured. "How long have we been out here, a couple of hours?"

"You might want to check your watch."

Shy fished her phone out of her pocket to check the time. "It's almost one," she said incredulously. "We've been out here for five hours?"

Jake pulled off her gloves and slapped them against her leg to shake off the dust and grit. "Time flies when you're having fun."

"That was pretty rad. It was hard work, but it was fun, too."

Jake locked the storage unit and climbed in the truck. "Which part? Unstacking the traps, rewiring them, ripping your sleeve on the new wire, or loading the trailer?"

Jake pressed her fingers through the jagged hole in Shy's sleeve to see if she needed to swing by Dr. Halloran's for a tetanus shot, but Shy's tawny skin appeared to be unscathed.

"All of it, but mostly being with you." Shy's cheeks reddened. Jake felt her own face warm in response as she reluctantly withdrew her fingers from the opening. "I liked showing you what I can do," Shy said with an almost palpable sense of accomplishment. "What's next?"

"If we break for lunch, we'd lose an hour of daylight. If you want to keep going, I tossed a couple of peanut butter and jelly sandwiches in the cooler this morning. We could eat those during the drive to the dock, finish our work, and make it an early day. I have some salmon steaks I could throw on the grill for dinner. I'm sure Kate and Tess would come over if I asked. Or we could make it quick and easy and pick up some takeout on the way home. It's up to you. I'm open either way."

Shy screwed up her face as if she wasn't used to being put in the position of having her opinion matter. "Let's keep going."

"Sounds good to me. The cooler's behind you."

Shy reached into the back seat, opened the cooler, and pulled out the sandwiches and two bottles of water. She opened the waterproof sandwich bags and the bottles of water and handed Jake one of each. She swallowed half her sandwich in one big bite, then asked somewhat self-consciously, "Is it always this much fun or am I just excited because it's my first day?"

Jake took a long drink of water and placed the bottle in one of the slots in the truck's dual cup holder. "It's all a matter of perspective. You can let me know how you feel when the salt water cracks your hands open but you're too frozen to feel the pain because it's only twenty degrees out."

Shy's jaw dropped, revealing a colorful mouthful of PB and J. "Seriously?"

Jake nodded. "The winter months are rough, but I usually shut down before conditions get too bad."

"Then you build boats."

"Ayuh. Then I build boats."

"I heard you working on your boat last night."

Jake had tried her best to be quiet, but the argument with Jeannie had left her furious and she'd wanted to take her anger out on something besides herself. "I didn't wake you, did I?"

"No," Shy said, but Jake suspected she was lying in order to spare her feelings. She almost asked Shy if she wanted to give her a helping hand sometime, but Shy would likely say no, and it was best they maintained a bit of professional distance anyway. She was not only Shy's supervisor but her landlord as well. Two really good reasons to keep her distance.

"I'll try to keep it down next time."

"No worries." Shy finished the rest of her sandwich and licked boysenberry jelly off her fingers. "May I ask you something?"

"Sure. What?"

"Is it okay if I have someone over to spend the night? Maybe even a weekend?"

Jake didn't think Shy had had time to find someone in Portland to hook up with. Or maybe she had spotted someone in the Watering Hole who had piqued her interest and she was planning for the future.

"You work fast."

"It's not like that. I was planning to invite a friend from home."

"One of the friends your family wants you to stay away from?"

Shy's expression darkened, and Jake saw a spark of anger in her eyes. Jake held up a hand to keep the spark from turning into a flame.

"It's your apartment. As long as you don't wreck the place, you can spend time there with whoever you want. You don't have to ask my permission."

"Cool."

Shy's broad grin was both infectious and incredibly attractive. Jake hoped whoever Shy was planning to welcome into her bed in the coming weeks would prove worthy of the invitation.

❖

Shy was sore. Every part of her body hurt. Even her hair. She felt every second of the hours of tedious work she and Jake had put in today. She wanted to collapse into bed and sleep for the next twelve hours, but she couldn't do that when she'd already agreed to have dinner with Jake, Kate, Tess, and Morgan.

Wincing with each step, she slowly descended the stairs and headed for Jake's back deck, where everyone else had already gathered. The evening was cool, but not too bad. The days were warming up nicely and so were the nights.

This morning, Shy had woken up to find frost on the ground. Tonight, the temperature was supposed to be around forty. Practically a tropical heat wave around these parts.

"I would ask you how your first day was," Kate said, "but I can tell it's kicking your ass."

"You have to put a dollar in the swear jar," Morgan said. "You said the a-s-s word."

"Like spelling it out is any better?" Tess asked. "For that, you get to put in a dollar, too."

"Aw, Mom."

Kate took a sip of her iced tea. "Don't whine, kid. Between the three of us, we'll soon have enough money in that jar to erase the national debt." She patted the chair next to her. "Take a load off, Shy."

"Where's Jake?"

"She's checking on something in the kitchen. Which gives you plenty of time to tell me how your day went." She poured Shy a glass of tea. "Jake wasn't too hard on you, was she?"

"No, she was…perfect. I expected her to bark orders at me all day, but she didn't raise her voice even once. She was patient enough to let me make mistakes and not too hard on me while I tried to figure out how to fix them."

"Learning from your mistakes is the best way to catch on," Kate said. "Learn fast. Once the fishing starts, Jake won't be able to hold your hand. You'll have to pull your own weight. Today was a practice run. Tomorrow's the real thing. Are you ready for it?"

"I hope so."

She got butterflies every time she thought about tomorrow. She had passed today's test, but tomorrow would be her first real chance to prove herself—or fall flat on her face. Tomorrow, the training wheels would come off. The boat would be out on the open water instead of tied safely to the dock. Shy didn't want to end up like the poor greenhorns she saw on TV, seasick and useless as they failed miserably at a job that was harder up close than it looked from afar.

She wanted to do a good job for Jake. She wanted to make her family proud of her. She wanted to be proud of herself. She couldn't accomplish any of her goals if she spent her first day at sea hanging over the side of the boat feeding the fish.

"Twenty bucks says you blow chunks," Kate said with a mischievous grin.

Shy had started to feel a little nauseous while the boat was moored at the dock today. She thought she'd be okay once she and Jake went out to sea, but she wasn't willing to bet on it.

"Don't listen to her," Tess said. "She gives all the greenhorns grief the night before they go out for the first time. You'll be fine."

Tess's maternal manner made Shy feel like part of the family. A good thing, considering her own family was over a hundred miles away.

"Are you enjoying your stay so far?" Tess asked.

"It's a lot different from what I'm used to."

"I can imagine. The change of pace must be jarring for you. Maybe not yet since there's been so much for you to do the past two days. But this weekend you'll have a chance to see what life here is really like."

"Careful, honey," Kate said. "You'll scare her into thinking all we do for fun is sit around watching paint dry."

"Hey, Mom, why don't you ask her if she can come to Pete's game this Saturday?" Morgan said enthusiastically.

"It was your idea," Tess said. "Why don't you do the honors?"

Morgan stammered as if he were asking Shy out on a real date. "Um, my brother's pitching against the Mets this weekend. Do you think you might want to come?"

"Only if you promise to snag a foul ball for me."

Morgan's freckled face lit up. "I'll be sure to take my glove."

"Then it's a date. Do you think Jake would like to come, too?"

"I doubt it," Morgan said. "She never goes anywhere fun."

"Why not?"

Morgan started to respond, but Tess silenced him with a look before she turned to Shy. "You'll have to ask her. It's her story to tell, not ours."

The comment reminded Shy of an old joke she had once heard about Southerners being so proud of their eccentric relatives that instead of hiding them away from the rest of the world, they put them on the front porch so everyone could see them. Perhaps New Englanders gave theirs the keys to a boat and sent them fishing instead.

"There you are," Kate said when Jake came out of the kitchen carrying a tray of raw salmon steaks. The marbled pink meat shining with marinade looked so good it made Shy's mouth water. "I was beginning to think you got lost in there."

Jake lifted the lid on the grill and dropped the steaks onto the heated metal grate one by one. "I was trying to get the timing down. Cooking for one's a lot easier than cooking for five."

"Do you need some help?" Shy asked.

"Not now, but I will in about five minutes," Jake said as she kept a close eye on the sizzling meat. "When the oven timer goes off, will you take the potatoes out and put them in a bowl? The oven mitt and a pair of tongs are on the counter. Butter, cheese, sour cream, and chives are in the fridge."

"I think I can handle that."

When the timer dinged and Shy stood to head to the kitchen, she heard Kate whisper to Tess, "I can already tell they're going to make a great team. If they work together this well on land, they're going to be a dream on the water."

Shy planned to do her best to make sure Jake's and Kate's confidence in her wasn't misplaced. Jake had taken a chance on her and she wasn't about to let her down. In turn, she wished Jake would let her in. Not forever. Just long enough to tell her the story Tess and Kate wouldn't share. The story of her life. Why did Jake have trouble sleeping? When she closed her eyes at night, was she tormented by visions of the one that got away, or had something more serious occurred to rob her of peace?

Shy wanted to know more about her mysterious new boss, but she would have to break through her own barriers to do it. She wasn't used to asking people to open up about themselves because she knew they would expect her to do the same. She didn't like talking about herself. She didn't like talking, period. Mostly because she didn't know what to say. Which was probably why she liked being around Jake so much. Conversation came easy with her even when they didn't say anything at all. When they were working today, they said only what was necessary to get the job done, not any of the mindless BS other people went on and on about to pass the time.

Shy smiled to herself as she realized she was becoming as protective of Jake as Rita, Kate, and Tess. She'd just met her, but she was already willing to have her back. Was it because Jake seemed like an underdog or did she have the potential to be something else? Something Shy didn't have many of: a true friend.

"Morgan invited me to go to the Sea Dogs game with him, Tess, and Kate this weekend," Shy said as she and Jake cleaned up after dinner.

"He seems to be developing a bit of a crush on you."

"I noticed. Don't worry, though. I won't let it go too far before I find a way to let him down easy."

"Good."

After a few minutes of silence broken only by the clattering of freshly washed pots and pans being put away, Shy said, "Do you want to come with us on Saturday?"

Jake looked at her out of the corner of her eye. "Did Tess put you up to asking me that?"

"No, it was my idea. You wear a Sea Dogs cap all the time. I thought you were a fan of the team."

"I am. I just—I have a thing about crowds."

"How big is the stadium?" Shy couldn't imagine a minor league ballpark being very crowded, no matter how rabid the fans.

"Hadlock Field holds over seven thousand."

"That's nothing. Fenway holds over five times that."

"Ayuh, and you won't catch me there, either. Go to the game and have a good time. I'll listen on the radio while I catch up on things around here. This place won't look after itself, you know."

Shy looked around at the immaculate house and grounds. As far as she could tell, the only thing left to do was sit back and admire what had already been accomplished.

"I might need some help cheering Morgan up after I tell him there's no chance for us."

Jake dried her hands on a dish towel. "Something tells me you won't have any problems. Someone as beautiful as you are must have a string of broken hearts in your past."

Shy was thrown by the compliment. She hadn't expected to receive it or to have it feel so good. Defying her natural inclination to look away, she met Jake's steady gaze. "The only heart I've ever broken is mine."

"What was her name?" Jake asked after a beat.

Shy didn't want to talk about her seemingly fruitless pursuit of a woman who might never feel the same way about her. But perhaps Jake had someone like that in her life, too.

"I'll tell you my sob story if you tell me yours."

Jake's face clouded over. "There's no need for both of us to end the night in tears. Someone's got to run the boat tomorrow. Speaking of which…"

Shy took the hint without forcing Jake to spell things out for her. The situation was already crystal clear. Jake had hired her to do a job, not make friends.

"It's getting close to my bedtime. I'd better turn in so I won't keep you waiting in the morning. Thanks for dinner. Maybe next time we can do it at my place."

She made the offer casually, not expecting Jake to take her up on it, but Jake surprised her by saying, "Tell me when and I'm there."

"How about next Saturday?"

"Sounds good."

Jake's matter-of-fact response was in direct contrast to Shy's growing excitement. Shy had never invited anyone over before because she had never had a place of her own to invite them to. Her life was changing so quickly she could barely keep up.

"Is there anything special I should do to prepare for tomorrow?"

Her uncle had told her to eat plenty of bread for breakfast each day before she went out so it could soak up the liquid in her stomach and she wouldn't get seasick. She thought his advice might be an old wives' tale, but she'd do anything to keep from puking in front of Jake, especially since Kate had already ribbed her about it.

"When I was freaking out over taking the captain's exam, my dad gave me the best piece of advice I've ever received: don't think too much. Just take everything as it comes and you'll be fine."

Jake made things sound so easy. She made them look that way, too. But life, Shy knew, was often harder than it looked.

CHAPTER SIX

Jake usually hated being proven wrong, and Shy had spent the past twelve hours doing just that. Shy hadn't got sick once during the trip, even when a pair of rogue waves nearly flipped the *Mary Margaret* on its side. She'd gone a little green around the gills the first time she reached into the bait bin, but she'd managed to stuff the pieces of whitefish into the traps without losing her lunch in the process.

"I can't remember the last time a greenhorn didn't heave on the first day," Jake said as she tied off at the dock. "You just cost me and Kate twenty bucks each."

"You bet against me?"

Shy looked surprised Jake hadn't taken her side. Instinct had told Jake to bet for Shy instead of against her, but Shy's inexperience had convinced her not to. Now she was out twenty dollars and had potentially upset the dynamic on the boat.

"I was playing the odds, and the odds definitely weren't in your favor."

"Since you and Kate didn't believe in me, who did? Was it Tess?"

Jake grinned. "Let's just say Morgan won't have any trouble being able to afford to buy you a hot dog and a soda at the game Saturday night."

"I knew I liked him for a reason. I might have to change my mind about breaking up with him."

Jake nodded. "If he stays as sweet and level-headed as he is now, he's going to make someone a damn fine husband one day. Pete, too. Kate and Tess have done a really good job with those boys. And I'd say that even if they weren't family."

"How long have Kate and Tess been together?" Shy asked as she and Jake headed to the truck to begin the journey home.

"Pete was seven, almost eight when they got together. And Morgan was still in Tess's belly. So a little over thirteen years."

Shy looked suitably impressed. "That's a long time. My parents were together for twenty years off and on before my dad died, but they were more off than on, so it was more like ten or fifteen."

"My parents are coming up on fifty. Their anniversary's in July."

"Fifty years? That's twice as long as I've been alive. Can you imagine being with one person for that long?"

"Not a chance."

Jake used to imagine finding the woman of her dreams and spending the rest of her life with her. Now she didn't want to force anyone to put up with her nightmarish hang-ups and insecurities.

"Me neither."

"Why not?"

"Most of the women I've been with are Portuguese with the tempers to match. We'd kill each other before one year was up, let alone fifty."

"Ayuh, you might be right."

Shy wrinkled her nose. "Is that a Maine thing or what?"

"What?" Jake took her foot off the gas and looked around for a local landmark that might have caught Shy's attention. The buildings nestled by the harbors near Commercial Street were breathtaking, but Shy was looking at her instead of them.

"Whenever I ask you a question and I assume your answer's going to be 'yes,' you say, 'ayuh,' instead. You didn't at first, but you must have gotten used to me or something because now you do it all the time."

"Ayuh, I guess I have."

Jake felt warmth begin to spread throughout her chest. Shy was right. She had grown on her. Jake hadn't expected it to happen so soon, but she was starting to look forward to spending time with her. To getting to know her. To watching her learn how to do a job she had apparently been born for. Jake had told herself not to get too close, but how could she stay away? They worked together all day and lived practically in the same house at night. How was she supposed to keep her distance when they were never more than a few feet apart?

"When is your friend coming to visit?"

"She didn't say. It could be tomorrow. It could be never. With Lucy, you never know."

"Ayuh, some women are like that."

"Ayuh, they sure are."

Jake tried but couldn't hold back her laughter. "It sounds funny when *you* say it."

"I've got news for you. It sounds funny when you say it, too."

"You're probably right."

Shy pointed to some of the seafood restaurants lining the waterfront. "When you bring in a catch, does it end up in those places or does it get shipped halfway across the country?"

"Probably a little bit of both. After the guys in the harbor quote me a price and pay me for my haul, I don't have any control over who they sell it to. I assume most of the catch stays local, but anyone can catch lobsters if they have the appropriate licenses, so some restaurants set their own traps to cut down on costs."

"And people have been fishing these waters for hundreds of years? Why haven't they gone dry by now?"

"They might have if the regulatory agencies hadn't stepped in to make sure the populations remain sustainable."

"So that's why we'll have to toss back the undersized ones and the egg-bearing females. It's not just about avoiding fines.

It's about making sure the industry survives, too. Now I get it. Uncle Cristiano used to go on and on about the time he spent up here and how influential Portuguese sailors were in the whaling industry in Provincetown. I used to zone out once he got on a roll. All I wanted was to get back to what I was doing at the time. Now I wish I'd paid more attention."

"It's not too late, you know. Have you talked to your family since you've been here?"

"I called Mama when I got off the train to let her know I made it okay, and I called later on to let her know I got the job, but I don't check in every day, if that's what you mean. She works such long hours. I don't want to bother her when she's trying to rest."

"I doubt she would mind the interruption. If I don't check in with my parents as soon as I reach the harbor, my mother starts blowing up my phone. If I don't answer, she drives down to the dock to make sure I'm okay. At the Watering Hole, Tess keeps track of each crew. The bell behind the bar? She rings it each time a boat makes it safely back to shore."

"And if they don't?"

"She rings it for each hand that's lost."

"Have you ever known someone who didn't make it back?"

Jake tapped her knuckles against the side of her head. "No, knock wood, but if I stay in the game long enough, I'm sure I will eventually."

"Is that why you'd rather build boats than run them? So you don't have to worry about the danger?"

Jake gripped the steering wheel so hard her knuckles cracked. "No matter what you do, you can never stop worrying about the danger."

She forced herself to loosen her grip. The danger she feared most wasn't found on the water but on land. She felt safe on the ocean. It was everywhere else she felt lost.

"I'll be careful," Shy said earnestly. "Do you think I could drive the boat sometime?"

For the next few months, the waters from the bay and beyond would be a minefield of traps, buoys, and ropes. Even experienced captains would have a hard time keeping their rudders from getting tangled in someone else's lines. But Shy showed such an affinity for fishing Jake didn't want to turn her down. Anyone could learn to fish, but those who fished for a living did so not because they wanted to but because they had to. It was in their blood. Jake could easily imagine Shy joining the fishing fraternity one day. Her skills were raw, but she was a natural.

"It would be good to have two experienced helmsmen in case something goes wrong. If I can find a stretch of open water on the way back from the fishing grounds, I'll let you have a few minutes in the captain's chair. Just don't get too comfortable."

"Sweet."

Jake remembered the hesitant version of Shy she had met only a few short days before. Someone who wasn't sure if she belonged or if she wanted to stay. Now it seemed like she never wanted to leave. Jake was beginning to feel the same way about her.

❖

Shy stared at the dozens of display panels spread across the front of the helm. Each of the instruments kept track of something, from the amount of fuel in the tank to the number of horsepower in the diesel engine, but she was interested in only one: the GPS unit that marked the position of the traps they had set the day before.

"There they are," she said when the first set of brightly colored dots appeared on the small screen.

"I'll haul them up and you check them out."

Jake cut back on the throttle, slowing the boat's forward motion. Shy put her hand on the windshield to keep her balance.

"Do you think they're all full?" she asked as Jake manned the controls of the hydraulic lift system they had used to haul the traps into the water the day before. Now it was time to see what—if anything—they had caught.

Jake snagged one of the plastic buoys bearing her license number and began to haul the attached trap out of the choppy water. A flock of screeching sea birds circled overhead, waiting to swoop down and grab any fish that might have wandered into some of the traps and would be tossed over the side during the sorting process.

"I know it's only superstition, but most crews believe the results of the first set of traps dictate how good the season's going to be. If the first string is full of keepers, the rest of them will be, too."

Shy adjusted the thick rubber gloves designed to protect her hands from the lobsters' snapping claws. She crossed her fingers as the first trap neared the surface of the water. When the trap broke the surface, she saw four lobsters crammed inside. She didn't see any with berry-shaped eggs on their backs or notches in their tails. When she measured their carapaces, all were above the three-and-a-quarter-inch minimum and below the five-inch maximum.

"Is that good?" she asked after she taped the keepers' claws shut and tossed them into the hold.

"What do you think?" Jake's smile was as wide as the rocky shore they had left behind. "If we manage two keepers per pot, we'll haul in a thousand lobsters today. A thousand pounds at eight bucks per pound. Does that sound good to you?"

Shy rebaited the trap and gave the thumbs-up to let Jake know it was ready to be lowered into the water. "We could make eight thousand dollars today?"

"Maybe more, depending on the final tally and total weight."

"Awesome."

They finished the string and moved on to the next. Some pots contained more lobsters than others, some fewer. At the end of the day, Jake's unofficial tally read one thousand one hundred twenty-five, and Shy's hand was sore from sharing high fives.

When they went to market, they could leave with a check for ten thousand dollars. For one day's work. If that wasn't enough incentive to push through the pain and fatigue that showed up at the end of the day and didn't always dissipate by the next morning, she didn't know what was.

"The guys at the fish market are in charge of the final count," Jake said as they turned for home. "When we offload, they'll sort the catch to make sure no undersized ones got past us."

"Then they'll count them, weigh them, and quote us a price, right?"

"Right. After a quick trip to the bank, we can get cleaned up and head to the Watering Hole to celebrate a successful and profitable first day." Jake scanned the horizon. The fog was rolling in over the gulf, though it wasn't as thick as it was this morning or was predicted to be tomorrow. "Ready to take the wheel?"

"Really? Right now?" When Shy had asked for a lesson, she hadn't expected Jake to comply so soon.

"What can I say? I'm in a good mood. Now get over here before I change my mind."

Shy slid into the chair Jake had vacated.

"This is the shift lever and this is the throttle," Jake said. "You use them to shift gears and change speeds. The steering wheel's purpose is obvious, but some of the other things you need to depend on aren't quite as easy to figure out."

Shy listened as Jake explained all the gauges, levers, buttons, and switches that had been such a mystery to her before. Then she took the wheel, awed by the realization that a forty-five-foot boat worth more than six figures was completely under her control. One wrong move and both the boat and the haul could end up at the bottom of the ocean.

What would her friends think if they could see her now? Would they congratulate her for finding something more constructive to do than hanging out and getting high? Or would they, like crabs in a barrel, latch on to her to make sure she didn't escape their shared dead-end existence?

She had wandered through life aimlessly, drifting from one day to the next with no real goal in mind. Out here on the open water, she felt something she had never felt before: a sense of purpose. She liked it.

❖

Jake kept track on her clipboard as the dealers at the fish market verified her catch. She gave a small nod of satisfaction when their final number matched hers. "Okay, let's talk price," she said, sticking her pen behind her ear.

Nathan Pickens, the dealer she did business with most often, pulled a handheld calculator from his pocket and tapped his meaty fingers against the keys. "Six bucks a pound. That's the best I can do," he said, turning the display toward her so she could see the final price.

"Six? I was expecting eight."

"You and everybody else. But with the catches this good and the lobster this plentiful, the prices are being driven down. Tomorrow, it could be even lower."

"So I've got to catch more to make more."

"And that would drive down the prices even more, which is great for me but bad for you. I've got more boats waiting to offload. Six bucks. Take it or leave it."

"I'll take it." Jake smacked her clipboard against her thigh in frustration. Today's take-home was good, but over two thousand dollars less than what she'd thought it would be. Instead of making a profit, this season could turn into a battle just to break even.

"Still feel like celebrating?" Shy asked after Jake deposited Nathan's check in the night drop at the bank.

Jake tried to be positive to keep from lowering Shy's high spirits. Despite the final outcome, today was a good day. It deserved to be treated as such.

"Let's do it."

After a pit stop at the house to shower and change, Jake drove to the Watering Hole. Tess rang the bell behind the bar as soon as she and Shy walked in.

"The *Mary Margaret*. Two bells and all's well," Tess said, letting everyone know the boat and her crew had returned safely to port.

The patrons in the bar raised their drinks to acknowledge the announcement. The show of camaraderie helped to improve Jake's outlook. The season was going to be difficult, but at least she wouldn't have to fight the battle alone. She would have a capable deckhand and a tight community by her side. The people in this room might not always understand her, but, to a man, they cared about her in their own way.

"The usual?" Tess asked after Jake and Shy found two seats at the bar.

Jake nodded.

"Same for me," Shy said.

Tess fished two bottles of Allagash from the cooler.

"To a good day of fishing," Jake said, raising her bottle in the air.

"And a successful season."

"I'll tell the kitchen to get dinner started," Tess said. "What'll you have, Shy?"

"Same as before."

"You, too, huh? Thanks for making my job easy." Tess entered the orders in the computer. "Ready for the big game tomorrow night?"

"I'm looking forward to it. I tried to get Jake to tag along, but she turned me down."

"Join the crowd."

Tess patted Jake's hand to let her know she wasn't harboring any hard feelings, but Jake could tell how much it would mean to her and the rest of the family if she'd change her mind. She looked away to avoid the yearning in Tess's eyes.

"Have you seen Charlie around? I haven't laid eyes on him or Jeannie since Wednesday."

"He was in earlier, flashing money like it was going out of style. He was three sheets to the wind when he came in and he got pissed when I told the bartenders not to serve him. He staggered out of here about an hour ago."

"So he did manage to hook up with Thorny's crew?"

"No, Thorny wouldn't hire him, either. In fact, Thorny told him not to come back until he could prove he'd been clean for at least a month." Tess lowered her voice. "I heard Charlie say Jeannie got a loan from your parents to keep them afloat for a while."

Jake took off her cap and ran her hands through her hair. "I was afraid that would happen."

Her parents were retired and living on a fixed income. They didn't need to be dipping into their savings to lend money they'd never get back. But Charlie had probably convinced Jeannie he could get clean and she had convinced their parents to lend her the money. Now a good chunk of it was in Charlie's hands and he was partying all over town. In a few weeks, the cycle would begin again.

Jake knew she couldn't solve everyone's problems—hell, she couldn't even solve her own—but she couldn't stop trying to figure out a way to make everyone happy.

"Have you tried an intervention?" Shy asked.

Jake shook her head. "Interventions don't work unless the addict is willing to accept responsibility for the effect his actions have on the people around him and admit he needs help. Charlie isn't there yet. Even though I finally convinced myself to turn him loose and separate myself from the situation, I'm still right in the middle of it."

"Tess is right. You can't save everyone."

"I know." Jake thought of Susan and the fear she'd seen in her eyes that fateful April day two years past. "Believe me. I know."

CHAPTER SEVEN

Shy lowered herself into her seat in the pavilion above the right field wall. In left field stood the Maine Monster, painted green to match the wall at Fenway. Game time was still thirty minutes away, but Hadlock Field was already packed. Singles, couples, and whole families filled the seats.

On the field, the visiting Binghamton Mets and the hometown Sea Dogs were completing their final warm-ups. The seventy-three hundred fans in attendance were buzzing with anticipation. If they won tonight's game, the Sea Dogs would move into first place in the Eastern League. The team's mascot, Slugger the Sea Dog, ran up and down the aisles waving his arms for more noise. First place was a cause to celebrate, to be sure, but the signs circling the stadium revealed the team hadn't won the league title or double-A championship in nine years.

"See number five?" Morgan asked, pointing to a Sea Dogs pitcher loosening up in the bullpen below them. "That's my brother, Pete."

The catcher's glove popped each time he corralled one of Pete's pitches. Shy didn't have a speed gun, but she was willing to bet Pete's fastball topped out near a hundred. His curveball moved like Carmen Miranda's hips dancing a samba. He had power and finesse, but it wouldn't matter if he didn't have control, too. According to the stats in the program in her hands, he led the team in both strikeouts and walks. He also led the team in wins, a stat he added to after he pitched nine shutout innings in a 2-0 Sea Dogs victory.

"Wasn't that great?" Morgan asked as they waited for Pete to emerge from the locker room after the game.

The game wasn't pretty—there were more errors than hits for the first few innings—but it had been exciting the whole time.

"Ayuh, it sure was."

Morgan laughed and said, "You're starting to sound like Mama Kate and Cousin Jake," which drew chuckles from Tess and Kate as well.

Shy felt honored to be included in such distinguished company. "Thanks."

"There's a day game tomorrow. Would you like to come to that one, too?"

"Morgan," Tess said, "you know Kate and I can't come to tomorrow's game. We already made plans to visit the artists' colonies on Monhegan Island."

"You don't have to come. It could just be me and Shy," he said as if he'd just come up with the idea. "Right, Shy?"

Shy smiled inwardly at Morgan's not-so-subtle maneuverings. He reminded her of her little brother. Like Federico, Morgan's soft, boyish features were becoming more angular, providing a glimpse of the man he would soon become. She remembered Jake's comment about Morgan making someone a good husband one day. It seemed he was trying to put himself in position to become hers right now. She would set him straight before things got too far. Until then, she could have a few laughs with him and his moms and, perhaps, make a few friends in the process.

"I'd love to."

"I suppose you'll be inviting her to Palace Playland next," Kate said.

"What's that?" Shy asked.

"An amusement park right on the beach," Morgan said excitedly. "It's up in Old Orchard Beach and it has everything:

thrill rides, roller coasters, a Ferris wheel, and arcade games, too. They've got a carousel and a bunch of stuff for little kids, but I like to go on the real rides—Drop Zone, Adrenalin, and Matterhorn. Power Surge is my favorite, though. The guys running the ride strap you into it with a harness over your shoulders, but your legs get to hang free. When the ride starts, you rotate around the main arm and your seat spins every which way. It's awesome."

"Admission is free," Tess said, "but you have to buy tickets for each ride. That's how they get you."

"How much do tickets cost?" Shy asked.

"A buck twenty-five apiece," Kate said. "The most popular rides cost three or four tickets, so we usually buy Morgan a book of twenty and call it a day. When Pete was younger, the two of them would burn through fifty tickets a trip."

"How often did you go?"

"As often as possible. They practically lived there during the summer. Now, not so much."

"It's not as much fun without Pete around," Morgan said.

He looked disconsolate as he pounded his fist in his glove so Shy tried to cheer him up.

"Power Surge sounds like fun. Maybe you could take me to see it sometime. I've never been to an amusement park on the beach before."

"I'll call you," he said with a practiced smoothness.

Shy ruffled his hair. "You do that, Romeo."

Morgan's precocious display of maturity disappeared as soon as he saw his brother walking across the infield. "Pete!" he called out, his voice at least two octaves higher than normal.

His shoulders slumped and his gait glacial, Pete didn't bear the look of a man who had just led his team to victory. His hangdog expression matched the one that had been on Morgan's face a few minutes earlier.

"What's wrong, son?" Tess asked, rubbing a soothing hand against his scraggly beard.

Pete sighed heavily. "Coach asked to see me after the game."

"What did he want?" Kate asked apprehensively.

"He sat me down and told me I'd just played my last game for the Sea Dogs."

"What? You got cut?" Morgan pulled off his glove and hurled it to the ground. "That's bullshit."

"It's okay, bro. Let me lend you a dollar for the swear jar." Pete reached into his gym bag and pulled out a brand-new Pawtucket Red Sox cap.

Tess gasped as Morgan stared at his new possession. "Does this mean what I think it means?"

Pete broke into a grin. "I'm moving up to triple-A. One stop away from The Show."

Kate and Tess showered Pete with hugs and kisses. When they were done, they invited Shy to go to dinner with them to celebrate Pete's good news, but she didn't want to intrude on time meant to be spent with family. Their closeness made her homesick.

It sounded weird, but she missed arguing with her mother and squabbling with her brothers and sister. She even missed her uncle and his corny stories about the good old days.

She missed Lucy, too, and the rest of her friends. She wondered if they were having a good time at Hector's party. Who would be the first to get drunk, break something, and cause Hector to kick everyone out? Probably Carolina. She couldn't hold her liquor no matter how hard she tried. And, man, did that girl try.

As she sat in her apartment trying to watch TV, Shy thought about buying a ticket home to pay everyone a visit in a few weeks, but she quickly decided against it. Once she got to Boston, she knew how hard it would be to turn around and come back. Yeah, it was nice here, but it wasn't home. And as nice as the Myerses were, they weren't her family. Sometimes, though, they damned sure felt like it. Especially the night before the season started. They had sat on Jake's back deck, laughing and talking easily with her like they'd known her for years.

Shy wasn't used to being made to feel so welcome. When the season ended, she was going to have a hard time saying good-bye. If she did a good job, maybe Jake would invite her back next year. She hoped so. She could easily see this becoming an annual thing.

She wished Jake had been in the stands to see the game and on the field to hear Pete's announcement afterward. She felt sorry for her in a way. How much was she missing out on by working on the boat all day and locking herself in her woodshed all night? She had a good life, but it seemed incomplete.

"Like I'm one to judge."

Her life in Southie was beginning to feel like part of a different world. Here, she didn't feel like an outsider. Even though she was surrounded by faces much paler than hers, she was starting to feel like she belonged. She didn't want the feeling to end.

❖

It was after midnight when Jake got home. The Watering Hole didn't close until three a.m. on the weekends, and she was sure the celebration for Pete's promotion to triple-A would keep going until then. She'd listened to Mike Antonellis's call of the game on WPEI while she worked on the sloop she was building. When Tess had called with the good news and invited her to an impromptu party at the Watering Hole, she had expected to see Shy there when she arrived.

"She asked Kate to take her home after the game," Tess had said. "You probably passed them on your way here."

Jake didn't know why she had felt so disappointed. As best she could figure, she'd gotten so used to spending sixteen hours a day with Shy, she didn't know what to do when they were apart. Except the explanation didn't make sense. Normally, her favorite part of the season was the weekend. Being able to get away from everyone and everything and be by herself for a while. Not this year. This year, she wanted to spend more time with her greenhorn, not less.

Jake smiled as she thought of how quickly Shy latched on each time she showed her something new. How to repair traps. How to load bait. How to drive the boat. She'd be wanting to work the hauler next. Just like everything else, she'd probably be good at that, too. If Shy decided to stick around, Jake thought they would make a hell of a good team. In more ways than one.

"You're getting too close," Jake warned herself after she parked her truck in the garage and her eyes inexorably drifted to the lights in the apartment windows a floor above. She forced herself to walk toward her front porch instead of the back stairs. "Don't start something you can't finish."

She headed inside for a few hours' sleep bound to be made more restless by her unwelcome realization that Morgan wasn't the only member of the Myers clan with a crush on Shy.

Chapter Eight

Shy deposited her paycheck into her account and withdrew one hundred dollars in cash. "See you next Friday, Rita."

Rita paused to wave as she waited on a customer. "Have a good weekend, Shy. You, too, Jake."

"Tell Andy hello for me," Jake said.

"Ayuh, I sure will."

"Can we stop by the market on the way home?" Shy asked on their way out of the bank as she tucked her cash and deposit receipt into her pocket. "I want to pick up a few things for tomorrow night's meal."

Jake climbed into the truck. "Save your money. I'm already deducting for groceries and utilities. I can pay for whatever you want to pick up today."

"No, you've already paid for enough. You pick up the tab for dinner every time we go out to eat. I've got enough hours under my belt. It's time I started pulling my own weight. This meal's on me."

Jake shrugged. "If you insist."

After Jake drove her to the grocery store, Shy grabbed a shopping cart and began to walk up and down the narrow aisles. She didn't know what she wanted to make for tomorrow night's dinner, but she knew she wanted it to be special. Jake had been good to her. Taken a chance on her when others might not have. Shy wanted to show her how much she appreciated the opportunity she had been given.

She picked up a bagged salad and a bottle of dressing. That part was easy. It was the entrée that had her stumped. Should she go with seafood, which was fresh and plentiful, or should she take a chance on something Jake might not have tried before? When she saw the rib eyes in the display case, she knew exactly what to make.

She grabbed a pack of thin-cut rib eyes, two bottles of red wine, two large potatoes, and a small carton of eggs. Together, the ingredients would become steak with an egg on horseback. She'd fry the steaks and potatoes, reduce one bottle of wine into a sauce for the meat, serve the potatoes on the side, and top each of the steaks with an egg served sunny side up.

The dish was a Portuguese delicacy and would offer her a chance to share a bit of her culture with Jake. Jake had been generous enough to welcome her into her world. Shy wanted to return the favor. Introduce her to Portuguese food, wine, and beer. Teach her folk dances like the Fandango, the Bailarico, and the Two Steps Waltz. Shy smiled as she pictured her and Jake on the dance floor, tripping over each other's feet as they tried to perform the intricate steps.

She started marinating the meat as soon as she got home and spent most of Saturday afternoon prepping everything else. She started laughing as she sliced the potatoes.

"You'd think I was getting ready for a date."

A date would begin with butterflies in her stomach and end, hopefully, with the mutual shedding of clothes and inhibitions. This wasn't a date. This was dinner. This wasn't a date. It was a thank-you. And yet it felt like so much more. It felt like the beginning of something, though Shy couldn't imagine what.

Yes, she and Jake were still in the beginning stages of their working relationship, but surely that was the only kind of relationship they would—or could—ever have. She had managed to find a place in Jake's world, but she doubted Jake would be able to find one in hers. The peaceful thoroughfares of Portland, Maine, were nothing like the mean streets of South Boston. Jake wouldn't last a day there, even with an escort. And, unlike Jake's family, who had welcomed her with open arms, Shy knew hers wouldn't exactly roll out the red carpet in return. No, Portland was where Jake belonged. She and her family were so ingrained in the fabric of the town, Shy couldn't imagine her making a life anywhere else. Could she, too, make a life here one day?

Jake knocked on the door at six thirty, half an hour before Shy planned to put dinner on the table. She wasn't wearing her usual uniform of jeans and a long-sleeved T-shirt. She was wearing a pair of charcoal gray slacks and a white button-down shirt instead. It took Shy a minute or two to figure out what else was different about her. Jake's ever-present Sea Dogs cap was missing, too. Her hair, normally covered, was combed into a style that showed off her high cheekbones and well-defined jawline. Her face was devoid of makeup, but her skin was so naturally pretty it didn't need artificial enhancement. To put it plainly, she looked hot.

"I'm not too early, am I?" Jake asked after Shy invited her inside. "I thought you might need a helping hand."

"No, I'm good." Shy took a moment to regain her lost equilibrium. "There's a bottle of wine open if you want to pour yourself a glass."

Jake poured two, one for each of them. She carried hers with her as she looked around the apartment. "I haven't been up here since the day you moved in. I like what you've done with the place."

Shy hadn't bought many accessories since she'd moved in. Just a few things that had caught her eye while she was wandering around town. A Slugger doll and a signed baseball she'd picked up at the Sea Dogs game, a coffee table book on actual sea dogs that explained the piratical origin of the team's name, and a miniature lobster boat carved out of driftwood.

"Where did you get these?"

Shy turned to see what had captured Jake's attention. Jake was standing in front of a set of vintage postcards Shy had placed in a frame. The cards were new, but the scenes on the front were almost two hundred years old. They depicted downtown Portland when the cobblestone streets were freshly laid, not worn smooth with age like they were now.

"I bought them from a shop in Old Port. As Time Goes By, I think it's called."

Jake nodded in recognition. "I know that place. The owner plays bridge with my mother twice a week, though I think they do more gossiping than bidding."

Shy grabbed two eggs out of the refrigerator and placed them on the counter so they would be within easy reach when the steaks were almost done. "Do you know everyone in town or does it just seem like it?"

Jake chuckled. "When I was younger, I would have loved a bit of anonymity. Since most of the moms in town knew mine, it was hard for me to get away with anything. If I did something wrong, the news made it home before I did."

"Yeah, I know what that's like. One time, my mother grounded me for missing curfew and I snuck out of the house while she was at work so I wouldn't miss the biggest party of the year. I was having the time of my life. The music was banging, I was chatting up a girl who was laughing at all my lines. Then, all of a sudden, everything got real quiet. And the girl I was talking to? Her eyes got real big like she'd seen something she wished she could forget. I didn't have to turn around to know my mother was standing behind me. Someone had called her and given her the heads-up about where I was. She dragged me out of the party by the scruff of my neck like I was a lost kitten or something. My friends have never let me forget it. They bring it up every time they want to bust my chops."

"That's what friends are for, aren't they? To get you through the bad times and to make sure you don't forget the good ones, even though some might not seem quite so good at the time."

Shy wondered who Jake turned to when she wanted to forget a bad experience or remember a great one. She had more acquaintances than Shy could count, but how many, if any, did she consider friends? The number was probably much smaller than Jake was willing to admit. One more thing she and Shy had in common.

Jake pointed at a picture of two women wearing old-fashioned bathing suits that covered more skin than they revealed. The picture reminded Shy of the time she and Lucy took the train to Atlantic City and posed behind one of those cardboard cutouts you stuck your face through. The cutout they had chosen featured two bathing beauties similar to the ones on the postcard. That's why she had bought it in the first place.

"That looks like Peaks Island," Jake said, looking closer. "In its day, it was known as the Coney Island of Maine. During the summer months, people used to flock there from all over to spend time in the hotels, theaters, and amusement parks."

"Did it have anything like Palace Playland?"

"Screaming kids, frustrated parents, and all the junk food you can eat. Some things never change."

"Amusement parks aren't your thing, huh?" Shy stirred the wine sauce to see if it was starting to thicken. "What do you do for fun?"

With her aversion to crowds, there couldn't be much fun stuff left to do. Especially in Maine.

"You already know what I like, don't you?"

Shy tasted the wine sauce to check the flavor. She liked a ton of spice in her food, but Jake's palate was probably tamer than hers so she'd dialed back. "I know you build boats, but that's for money, not fun."

"Actually, it's both." Jake came and stood next to her. "I never feel more grounded than when I'm constructing something made for the water. When I touch the curve of a finished hull, knowing I built it with my own hands, I feel a sense of accomplishment that's unmatched by anything else."

Shy imagined Jake running her hands over her curves. Slow and unhurried like they had all the time in the world instead of a few short months. She shivered despite the kitchen's heat. The small room felt even smaller when Jake brushed against her to take a closer look at the steaks.

"If I'd known you had such skills in the kitchen, I would have invited myself to dinner last week."

The scent of Jake's cologne, a light musk with a refreshing hint of citrus, filled Shy's lungs. "Don't give me too much credit. You haven't tasted any of the food yet."

Jake looked at her, a rare smile lighting up her face. "If it tastes as good as it smells, I'm in for a treat."

Shy was thinking the same thing.

Jake took a sip of her wine but didn't move away. "Are you sure there isn't anything you need me to do?"

I need you to kiss me.

The idea rose unbidden to the forefront of Shy's mind. The thought felt simultaneously like a revelation and a betrayal.

The Portuguese community in South Boston was small but close-knit. When she was little, her father had told her not to bring a boy home unless he was "one of us." After she told him she liked girls, the pronoun in his demand had changed, but his attitude had remained the same. So she had limited her dating options to the small pool of girls who fit her family's restrictions.

Her parents had been cordial to most of the girls she'd brought home to meet them, but neither was especially fond of Lucy, even though the Silvas and the Pereiras had been tight since Shy and Lucy were four years old. Shy didn't know if her family expected her to remain single for the rest of her life or become a nun. Neither being alone nor taking a vow of chastity held any appeal to her.

She had dated around the past few years, but she always kept going back to Lucy. Before he died, her father had tried to convince her to stop seeing Lucy, but Shy hadn't been able to fulfill his wish. Being with Lucy felt right, even though everyone around her tried to convince her it was wrong. Sometimes even Lucy.

What Shy felt when she was with Lucy, though, paled in comparison to what she was feeling now. She felt drawn to Jake in a way she had never felt before. She had never felt such longing. She didn't know what to do with the feeling. Should she embrace it or push it away?

The music wasn't helping. She had downloaded several songs by Amália Rodrigues and had them playing on her phone while she cooked. Rodrigues was known as the Queen of Fado, a type of Portuguese music characterized by mournful melodies and lyrics.

Shy had chosen fado as the soundtrack for dinner because most of the songs were about the sea. She thought Jake could relate to them, even if she might not be able to understand the words. But she had forgotten a very important thing. She had forgotten how the songs made you feel when you heard them. How they stirred up such deep-seated emotions in listeners, who were often moved to tears by the nostalgic tales of love and loss.

She felt stirred up now. But she didn't want to cry. She wanted to hold on to something—*someone*—she could never have.

"Why don't you get the salad ready?" she asked, trying to put some space between herself and Jake. "Then you can keep an eye on the potatoes while I fry up the steaks."

"That doesn't sound too hard."

Jake rolled up her sleeves and went to work with the same intensity she displayed when she was at the helm of the *Mary Margaret*. Between them, they pulled together a meal Shy would have doubted she was capable of if she hadn't been there to bear witness.

"You just raised the bar," Jake said after she'd taken the last bite of her steak. "I'll have my work cut out for me when it's time for me to return the favor."

Shy felt her face redden. Not at the compliment but at the notion she and Jake might make this intimate encounter more than a one-time thing. It could become a tradition like the grilled chicken sandwiches and sweet potato fries they ate every time they went to the Watering Hole. Though she wanted more nights like this, she wasn't ready for this one to be over.

They drifted to the living room after they washed dishes. Jake picked up the miniature lobster boat on the coffee table and turned it over in her hands. Shy wondered how the sculptor's craftsmanship compared to Jake's.

"How's your boat coming along?"

"Slow. I have months of work left." Jake carefully replaced the boat on its stand and shoved her hands in her pockets as if she were unsure of herself. "Would you like to see it?"

Shy quickly accepted an invitation rarely extended. "I'd love to."

Jake led her downstairs and to the woodshed out back.

"Don't you lock your door?" Shy asked after Jake opened the shed.

"I don't have to." Jake flipped the light switch next to the door and the twin fluorescent bulbs overhead flickered to life. "Portland's one of the safest cities in the country."

"Maybe, but this is Maine, not Mayberry. You've got a lot of nice things in here that could go missing."

Shy pointed to the worktable, which was lined with assorted hand and power tools. To Jake, the items were invaluable. To a thief looking for a quick payday, not so much. Television sets or DVD players, items that could be converted into quick cash, were more their speed.

"This is it." She removed the tarp covering her work in progress. "I think it's far enough along to give you an idea of where I'm going."

"Wow." Shy slowly circled the boat, which was still basically little more than a skeleton at this point. "What kind is it going to be?"

"A sloop. That's a sailboat with two sails. The mainsail and headsail are going to go here toward the front, but I have to build the mast and the boom before I can get started on those."

"And you're going to do all the work yourself?"

"It's not as hard as it looks."

"Right," Shy said, her voice dripping with sarcasm. "This isn't a balsa wood model kit you buy from the hobby store, Jake. It's the real thing. You're building an honest-to-God boat. Not many people can do that. I know I couldn't."

"You never know until you try."

And Jake thought Shy could do just about anything if she set her mind to it.

"Where would I find the time, the space, the tools, or the wood? Not in Southie, that's for sure." Shy circled the boat again. "What kind of wood are you using?"

"Teak. It's easy to work with and it resists water well so I won't have to add varnish when I'm done unless I want to change the color. If I leave it unvarnished, it will eventually fade to a nice silver-gray."

"It looks so smooth. Did you have to sand it?"

"Sanding would damage the wood. The summer growth bands on the surface are relatively soft and wear away on their own, especially on a deck or a porch. To maintain the boat, all I'll need to do is wash it in salt water and add more caulk to maintain its buoyancy."

"I wondered how you'd keep it from sinking."

Shy moved closer to the sloop but kept her hands at her sides despite her obvious curiosity.

"It's okay. You can touch it." Jake took Shy's hand in hers and guided it to the starboard side of the hull. "See what I mean?" she asked as she slowly slid their laced fingers along the smooth wood.

"Yeah," Shy said, her voice barely a whisper. "If I close my eyes, I can almost hear the ocean." She tightened her fingers around Jake's as she squeezed her eyes shut. "Do you hear it?"

Jake's heart hammered in her ears. When she closed her eyes, the sound almost passed for the ocean's roar. She took a deep breath, certain she could smell the salt air and feel the sun on her skin.

"Ayuh, I hear it."

Shy laughed. "Ayuh, I can, too."

Smiling, Jake opened her eyes. "Are you making fun of me again?"

Shy opened her eyes, too, but she wasn't smiling. "No, not this time." She turned her hand over. The hair on the back of Jake's neck stood on end as Shy's palm slid across hers. Shy's eyes glowed warmly as they gazed into hers. "What are you going to name her?"

"Who?"

"Your boat." Shy squeezed Jake's hand, then let go. "All boats are named for women, aren't they? What are you going to name yours?"

Jake's hands shook from a combination of adrenaline and arousal. She reached for the tarp to hide the tremors. "I haven't decided yet."

Shy grabbed the other side of the tarp and helped Jake drape it over the sloop. "How did the *Mary Margaret* get her name?"

"Kate named her for her great-grandmother on her mother's side, Mary Margaret Ferguson. She was an incredible lady. She meant a lot to Kate. I'll probably name my boat for someone who means as much to me."

"If you finish building it before I leave, will you take me for a ride?"

Jake could picture Shy sitting in the bow of the yet-to-be-named boat with the wind whipping through her hair and a glorious smile on her face as the full sails propelled them forward. If that wasn't the incentive Jake needed to finish the boat on time, she didn't know what was.

"You'll be my first passenger, I promise."

Chapter Nine

S hy had never been so cold. Rain had been falling steadily all day. Not the hard kind that felt like Mother Nature was subjecting you to twelve hours of the Chinese water torture, but the misty kind that seeped into your pores and sucked out your soul. The dark clouds overhead promised more of the same.

"If you don't like the weather in Maine," she had heard someone say while she stood in line at the bank one Friday afternoon, "wait a day." She couldn't wait for this day to end. Her teeth chattered as she counted keepers. Numbers had been steady for the first month of the season, but they'd started to take a nose dive this week and they didn't seem to be trending upward any time soon.

"How do we look?" she asked after she ducked inside the cabin to get out of the rain for a few minutes.

Jake checked her clipboard as she directed the boat toward the next string of traps. "We might make a thousand pounds today if the rest of the pots are packed. The way it looks now, though, we'll be lucky to make it to seven fifty."

"I know it's a long season, but how long can we keep going like this? We're making less money every day. Our numbers are down, and the market prices still are, too."

"I know. Kate called a few of her contacts to make sure the guys at the market weren't giving me the runaround with the prices. I did a little research of my own, too."

"And?"

"Prices truly are down. Lobsters are so plentiful, everyone's pulling in awesome numbers. We were, too, for a while and I know we will again if we're patient. What we do is called fishing, not catching, which means some days are better than others. Numbers fluctuate during the course of a season. It's not time to hit the panic button yet. Next week, we'll set the strings farther out in case the pods are migrating out to sea early. If we don't see improvement in a few weeks, I'll give my honey hole a try."

"Your honey hole? Is that like your super-secret fishing spot or something?"

"Ayuh. It's not as sexy as it sounds, is it?"

Shy felt the temperature in the cabin rise several degrees. Except for work, she and Jake hadn't spent any time alone since the night Jake had showed her the boat she was building. When Jake had taken her hand, Shy had been surprised at first. Jake wasn't the touchy-feely type, so her preferred method of contact was a handshake. Unlike her handshake, which was firm and businesslike, her touch that night had been gentle, the moment electric. But the moment had passed. Since then, she and Jake had resumed the roles Shy had been tempted to shed, that of captain and greenhorn. Jake gave the orders and Shy followed them. Just once, Shy wished the roles could be reversed. Or better yet, forgotten altogether.

What would it be like if she and Jake were on equal terms, not separated by rank, experience, or class? Shy could only imagine. Jake had never made her feel like she was little more than the hired help, but Shy's mother reminded her of the fact every time she spoke with her. "Be respectful," she said. "Stay in your place." The more Shy heard it, the less certain she became of where her place was. Was it in Boston with her friends and family or here on her own? Perhaps she'd figure it out one day. Until then, she had more important things to think about. Like improving the numbers so she could keep getting paid.

She adjusted her gloves as Jake approached the next string. Jake abandoned the captain's chair to stand next to the hauler, her cap worn inside out like a baseball player trying to spark a late-inning rally. Shy hoped the rally cap worked. She and Jake could use a win.

She peered over the side of the boat as a marked lobster pot slowly neared the surface. She felt like she had when she and Jake pulled their first pot of the season, anxious for good numbers. Just like that first pot, this one was also full of keepers, too. If only they'd remain that way for the rest of the year.

After the last string of pots was emptied and rebaited, Jake turned over the wheel like she did for a few minutes every afternoon. Shy slid into the captain's chair so she could operate the boat. She scanned the water in front of her for potential obstacles the way Jake had taught her. If struck hard enough or at the right angle, floating debris could damage the boat's hull. And Shy doubted it would take an iceberg to sink this *Titanic*.

"How was your weekend?" Jake asked, finally able to focus on something other than the catch now that the work day was almost over.

"It was fine until Morgan broke up with me."

"*He* broke up with *you*?"

Shy smiled at the memory.

"I went to Palace Playland with him and his moms on Saturday. The rides were even better than he said they would be. We'd just gotten off the Galaxi Coaster when Morgan took me aside and said he needed to talk to me. He said he'd given it some serious thought, but he and I needed to go our separate ways."

Jake laughed for the first time in days. Shy had missed the sound. "Did he say why?"

"I've seen the way Cousin Jake looks at you," he had said, "and I don't want to stand in her way."

Shy watched the waves breaking across the bow. She hadn't known what to say to Morgan then and she didn't know what to say to Jake now.

She didn't want to betray Morgan's confidence, partially because she didn't know if what he had claimed was true. Jake had never been anything but professional with her at work and cordial at home. Shy thought she had sensed a brief flicker of interest from her that night in the shed, but she hadn't felt it since. If she made a play for Jake and Jake turned her down, the long silences on the boat could swiftly turn from comfortable to awkward. If Jake didn't kick her off the *Mary Margaret* altogether.

Shy needed this job so she could help support her family. She liked helping her mother make ends meet. She could tell the money she sent home each week was starting to make a difference. The bill collectors had stopped calling, and her mother didn't seem nearly as worn down when Shy talked to her on the phone. Soon, they might be far enough ahead that her mother could work only one job instead of three. But until that day came, Shy couldn't risk her future on a few seconds, no matter how charged.

"It was one of those 'It's not you. It's me' situations," she said.

Jake scanned the water. "Maybe he has his eye on one of the girls at school."

"Maybe." Shy started when she heard something thump against the boat's rounded hull. "What the hell was that?" The boat quickly lost forward momentum and began to drift. Shy checked the gauges but didn't see anything out of the ordinary. She turned to Jake, who was monitoring the display panel as well. "What's wrong?"

Jake bolted out of her seat and threw open the cabin door. "Cut the engine. I think we've got something stuck in the rudder."

Shy quickly flipped the switch that cut power to the engine. "Did I do something wrong?" she asked as she followed Jake onto the deck.

"No, it could have happened to anyone. I was right there with you, remember? I didn't see anything, either."

Shy thought Jake was just trying to make her feel good by downplaying her screw-up, but she appreciated the effort. "So what do we do, drift until help arrives?"

"No, we solve the problem ourselves."

Jake peered over the side of the boat, then began to pull scuba equipment out of the compartment that housed the rain and survival gear.

"You're not going in, are you?" Shy asked after Jake took off her boots and jeans and began to pull on a wet suit and flippers. "You'll freeze. The weather guy on TV said the water's only fifty-seven degrees today."

Jake strapped an oxygen canister to her back and dipped a pair of goggles into the water before she settled them into place over her eyes. "We can't radio for the Coast Guard every time something goes wrong. That's one call I save for emergencies only. Hopefully, this isn't one." She grabbed a knife and strapped it to her thigh. "I'm going to go down and take a look."

"But we're in the middle of the ocean. What about sharks?"

"Sharks are cold-blooded creatures. The waters around here aren't warm enough for them yet. They'll be sunning themselves down in the Keys for a few more months. If I had to make this dive in August, I'd be a bit more worried about it than I am now."

Shy didn't buy her explanation.

"If there are no sharks around, what's with the knife?"

"I need to cut away whatever obstruction I find."

"What do you think it is?"

"It could be anything. Seaweed, plastic, and rope are the likeliest suspects. I just hope we shut the engine down in time before whatever it is wrapped too tightly around the propeller. If we didn't, I could be down there a while."

"What do you want me to do?"

Jake checked the gauge attached to the oxygen canister to see how much air remained in the tank.

"If I'm not back in half an hour, then you can radio for help. Try one of the other fishermen first. If no one's nearby, reach out to the Coast Guard as a last resort."

"I can do that."

Jake inserted the regulator in her mouth, gave a thumbs-up signal, and let herself fall backward into the water.

Shy felt helpless as she watched Jake disappear beneath the surface. Helpless and alone. She knew how to radio for help if she needed to, but she hoped she wouldn't need to. She didn't know what she would do if something happened to Jake. She wouldn't know how to begin to explain it to the ones Jake would leave behind. She wouldn't know how to explain it to herself.

"Please be okay. Please be okay," she whispered over and over again as the minutes slowly ticked by. She grabbed a flare to have something to hold on to and kept her eyes on the water, desperate for Jake to reappear.

The rain picked up, falling straight down at first like the ice-cold spray from a showerhead. Then the wind began to gust, driving the rain sideways. Shy turned her head so the rain could slide off her slicker instead of pelting her in the face. She shivered as her body temperature began to drop. Her mind tried to convince her to go inside the cabin so she could stay warm and dry while she waited for Jake to finish her work and return to the deck, but her heart wouldn't let her leave her post. Jake's safety came first, her comfort a distant second.

After the longest thirty minutes of Shy's life, Jake's head finally broke the surface. Jake spit out her regulator and pointed out the reason for the delay. Several lengths of rope were draped across her body like a bandolier, their ends sliced through.

"Someone set too close to our string," she said as she bobbed in the water. "That explains why our numbers have been down, even though everyone else's are so good. The rope to one of the other boat's buoys must have broken free from a pot. It wrapped itself around the propeller. It was wedged in there pretty good, but I managed to cut it loose." She grabbed hold of the side of the boat and tossed the pieces of rope on deck. "I didn't see any damage to the boat, so we should be good to go."

Shy dropped the rope into the storage compartment to keep it from getting in someone else's way, then helped Jake climb back onto the deck. Jake was so tired from her time in the water she could barely pull herself on board. She sank to her knees after Shy helped her remove her oxygen tank. She kicked off her flippers and remained on all fours for a few moments to catch her breath, the rain bouncing off her neoprene suit and her arms trembling with exhaustion. Just when Shy was starting to worry, Jake slowly pulled herself to her feet.

Once she was sure Jake was going to be okay, Shy impulsively threw her arms around her and gave her a hug. Jake stiffened in surprise, then relaxed and returned the pressure. When she finally let go, Shy noticed Jake's face was flushed. From excitement or exertion, she couldn't tell. She touched a gloved hand to one of Jake's rosy cheeks.

"Don't do that again, okay?"

"I didn't plan on doing it this time." Jake leaned against Shy's palm for a second before she pulled away. Her demeanor all business again, she jerked her chin toward the cabin as the rain petered to a stop. "Why don't you hit the starter and get us out of here?"

Shy hesitated. "You still trust me to drive after what I just did? I almost left us stranded."

Jake put her hand on Shy's shoulder and gave it a consoling pat. "Like I said before, it could have happened to anyone. You didn't do anything wrong, so stop beating yourself up about it, okay?"

Shy headed to the cabin but turned around before she made it to the door. "Thanks, Jake."

"For what?" Jake paused as she towel-dried her sopping wet hair.

"For believing in me."

Jake smiled reassuringly and playfully snapped at Shy's leg with the towel. "Take us home."

Shy started the engine and turned the wheel toward the shore. "You got it, Cap."

CHAPTER TEN

Jake wanted to cook the lamb chops on the grill and serve dinner on the deck because she loved being outdoors even when she wasn't getting paid to be, but the driving rain precluded any outside activities. Frankly, she was surprised Shy didn't need a rowboat to make her way from the garage to the house.

"It is some kind of nasty out there," Shy said as she dropped her dripping umbrella into the holder by the front door.

Jake helped Shy with her raincoat. "Is this what they call a wicked pissah back in Southie?"

"Your Boston accent is even worse than my Maine one," Shy said with a laugh.

Jake laughed, too, but only for a second because, simply put, Shy took her breath away.

Instead of the jeans and sweatshirt she usually wore both at work and at home, Shy was dressed in a pair of black slacks and a form-fitting silk sweater. The sweater was red. Not glaring like a stop sign, but rich and vibrant like a roaring fire on a cold winter's night. Its V-neck collar plunged dangerously close to Shy's cleavage, hinting at the rise of her breasts without giving too much away.

Jake wanted to press Shy against the wall, reach under the sweater, cup Shy's breasts in her hands, and feel the nipples harden against her palms. She wanted to watch Shy's eyes darken with desire, see her lips part, and hear her moan for more.

Jake was startled by the force of her attraction. Her libido had been in hibernation for months. Tonight, though, it was wide-awake. Unfortunately, she didn't know how she was supposed to proceed. She and Shy were working together, not seeing each other. Tonight was a meal, not a date. The last time they'd had dinner like this, though, they had ended the evening on an unexpectedly intimate note. Jake had shared more of herself that night than she'd expected she would. Shy had, too. Like that enticing hint of cleavage, Jake wanted to see more.

She hadn't been in a relationship in so long she didn't know if she was still capable of sustaining one. She and Susan had been together for almost three years before their time together came to an abrupt end. Jake had been stuck since then. Frozen on the last day she and the world around her felt normal. Being with Shy made her feel alive. Made her feel like it was okay to remember all the things she kept trying to forget. But how could she build a future with someone when she couldn't stop reliving the past?

"You look nice tonight," she said as she hung Shy's rain slicker on the coat tree. Though she was determined to keep the evening platonic, she didn't think one compliment would hurt. The resulting smile on Shy's face made the risk worth the reward.

"Thanks. You do, too."

Jake looked down at the khaki pants and navy blue fisherman's sweater she had decided to wear. She hadn't put much thought into the outfit. It had just felt right. Exactly how being with Shy was starting to feel.

"Something smells good," Shy said, sniffing the air. "What's for dinner?"

"Grilled lamb chops and sautéed asparagus," Jake said as Shy followed her through the house. In the kitchen, she dropped sliced mushrooms into the sauté pan and stirred them in with the asparagus spears. "I have to make sure you get enough protein to keep your engine running."

"You sound like my uncle. One of the reasons he started his food truck was so the kids in the neighborhood could have something affordable to eat besides fast food."

"When was the last time you talked to your family?"

Shy took a seat at the breakfast bar where Jake typically drank her first cup of coffee each morning while she read the headlines in the *Press Herald*.

"I call my mother every Saturday morning, but our conversations don't last very long. She works two full-time jobs and a part-time one, so she doesn't have much down time. When I call, I let her know that I'm okay and she brings me up to date on the goings-on at home. Then she catches a few hours' sleep before her next shift. Sometimes, she falls asleep in the middle of our conversation. I don't mind. I keep talking until I've said all I have to say. Most of the time, I just sit and listen to her breathe. It's almost like being back at home. The next weekend, we do it all over again." Shy's cheeks colored. "Each time we talk, she says she's proud of me."

"I am, too," Jake said as she took the food off the heat and pulled two dinner plates out of the cabinet.

Shy pushed her chair away from the breakfast bar. "So I'm doing a good job?" she asked as if she were afraid to hear the answer.

Jake was surprised Shy had asked the question because she thought the answer was obvious. Perhaps what was clear to her wasn't quite as clear to Shy. She turned to face her.

"I'm typically generous with encouragement and spare with praise because that's the way all the captains I've ever worked for treated me. I'm used to breaking balls, not giving pats on the back. You're doing a great job, Shy. I apologize for not having said so earlier."

"It's okay," Shy said with a grateful smile. "You don't say much when we're on the boat. I know you warned me it would be that way, but sometimes…" She paused, her smile faltering as she slowly lifted one shoulder in a shrug. "Sometimes, I can't tell if you like me or not."

Jake thought the answer to that question was pretty obvious, too.

"I do like you," she said, trying to keep the moment light, "but your feelings for me might change if dinner isn't up to snuff."

"I doubt that. You're great at everything you do." Shy's expression was so serious it made Jake's attempt at levity seem terribly out of place. She took a step closer. "May I ask you something?"

Jake's mouth went dry as she felt herself grow wet. Her attraction to Shy was growing by the day, and whenever she reflected on the night in the shed, she allowed herself to think perhaps the feeling was mutual. She had seen interest in Shy's eyes that night. Heard it in her voice. Felt it in her touch. Tonight the interest had returned and maybe, just maybe, Jake could compel herself to act on it instead of convincing herself it didn't exist.

"Sure," she said. "Fire away."

"I've been seeing flyers all over town about the Old Port Festival. Is it as big a deal as it seems?"

"It is around here."

"Have you been?"

"Not in the last few years." Jake grabbed a serving spoon and began to pile her plate with food to avoid talking about the past.

"What about this year?" Shy asked. "The festival's next weekend. Are you planning to go?"

Jake felt her pulse begin to race. The Old Port Festival was an annual event that took place on the second Sunday in June. Crowds grew larger and larger each year as locals and visitors alike turned up to celebrate. She swallowed hard as she imagined the thousands of people who would fill the streets next weekend. The same ones that would most likely return in August for the Maine Lobster Festival.

"I wasn't planning on it. Why? Do you want me to go with you?"

Shy hesitated as she reached for the remaining lamb chops in the grill pan. "Not exactly. I was telling Lucy about it and she said she wanted to go. I wanted to ask you if I could borrow your truck."

"Oh." Jake didn't feel the relief she had expected. She hadn't wanted to disappoint Shy by saying no to her invitation. Now she felt her own disappointment: at not having the opportunity to say yes. "Lucy finally agreed to come visit you?" she asked as she led the way to the dining room.

"When we were talking last night, she said I sounded homesick. She thought spending time with someone from the neighborhood would make me feel better." Shy pulled out a chair and spread her napkin in her lap. "She's coming up next weekend. I offered to take her to the festival because it sounded like fun. Since you have a thing about crowds, I never imagined you'd want to come, too. You can join us if you want. It might be fun."

Jake chewed mechanically, her appetite suddenly nonexistent. "I wouldn't want to intrude on your time with your...friend."

Shy had never defined her relationship with Lucy so Jake wasn't certain of the proper term to use. Shy's obvious excitement about Lucy's impending arrival, however, let Jake know the word she had finally chosen didn't provide an apt description. The way Shy's eyes glowed in the candlelight when she talked about Lucy, Jake could tell she was much more than a friend.

"May I borrow your truck this weekend? I promise to bring it back in one piece."

Shy was filled with so much nervous energy she couldn't sit still. Jake couldn't remember ever seeing her so excited. The only other time she had seen her nearly as engaged was when Jake had gotten her talking about the Red Sox. But the joyous look Shy had displayed while she listed her favorite players paled in comparison to the expression she was wearing now. She looked like a woman in love.

"Don't worry about the truck. It already has so many dents and scratches, one more won't hurt. Go to the festival and have a good time."

"Thanks, Jake." Shy's smile lit up the room. "I figured I'd take Lucy to the Watering Hole for dinner Friday night so I can introduce her to everyone. I'll show her around town on Saturday and we can spend Sunday afternoon at the festival. Her train leaves first thing Monday morning, so we can drop her off at the station before we head to the pier. She'll probably be back in Boston before we pull in our first string."

"Sounds like you have a full weekend planned."

"It took Lucy so long to decide to come up here, she gave me plenty of time to figure out what I wanted to do."

"What was the holdup?"

"She couldn't scrape up the cash for train tickets. She tried, but every time she got her hands on some extra dough, something unexpected came up and she had to spend the money on something else. Last week, I went down to the station and bought the tickets myself."

"You did? Why?"

"Round-trip tickets between Boston and Portland are only fifty bucks, so they didn't put too big of a dent in my budget."

"Do you always pay her way?"

"Not all the time, but I like doing nice things for her when I can afford it. Right now, I can afford it."

Even though Jake didn't know Lucy, she found herself questioning her motives. Had she finally agreed to come to Portland because she wanted to see Shy or because she wanted to see what she could get out of her now that Shy had a little money in her pocket? She hoped Lucy's feelings for Shy were as genuine as Shy's appeared to be for her. Shy didn't trust easily. Jake hated the idea that Shy's trust could be betrayed, especially by someone who obviously meant so much to her.

Shy pushed her empty plate away from her and skillfully changed the subject. "What are you going to do this weekend, work on your boat some more?"

"Ayuh, I suspect I will."

Tonight, though, Jake mentally prepared herself to spend yet another night alone. This time, not by choice.

CHAPTER ELEVEN

Shy stood in the enclosed waiting room in the Station Building inside the Portland Transportation Center with a bouquet of flowers in her hand. Lucy was due to arrive at seven thirty-five on the five o'clock train from Boston. According to the schedule overhead, the train was on time, which meant Lucy should be pulling into the station in less than five minutes. She called home to pass the time while she waited.

Federico answered the phone. "Since you're making all this money now," he said with the wheedling tone he always assumed when he worked his way into asking for something he knew he might not get, "you can afford to buy me a pair of Air Jordans for my birthday, right?"

"Why would I waste two hundred bucks on sneakers you'll only be able to wear for a month or two before you grow out of them? I'd be better off buying you a pair of no-names from the discount store."

Shy smiled as she listened to her little brother complain about never getting to wear anything except hand-me-downs. He sounded so pitiful she almost broke down and confessed she had already bought the shoes and planned to mail them to him the week before his birthday, but she didn't want to ruin the surprise.

"Freddy, quit your whining and put Mom on the phone."

"Mama, it's Shy," Federico yelled—mostly in Shy's ear, since he didn't bother to move his mouth away from the receiver. "She wants to talk to you."

"I have good news," her mother said when she finally came on the line.

"What?"

"I put in my notice at the *bodega*. I told Jaime I don't need the hours anymore."

"That's great, Mama. That frees up your weekends. Maybe you can give up the diner next. Then you can get some real sleep instead of catching a quick cat nap here or there."

Her mother chuckled. "You used to like me working long hours because it meant you could invite Lucy over and make out with her when you were supposed to be babysitting your sister and brothers."

"Times change, Mama. People do, too."

"Not some people. Lucy's just as selfish now as the day she was born. She probably will be until the day she dies." Shy's mother sucked her teeth in disapproval. "Are you sure inviting her to visit you is a good idea? I don't want you to spend so much time partying with her that you'll be too hung over to go to work on Monday. She drinks like a fish, you know. And I won't even mention the drugs. The bag of pills I found in your room that time. You claimed it was yours, but it was hers, wasn't it?"

Even though it would have cleared her name, Shy couldn't bring herself to snitch on Lucy. "That's ancient history, Mom. Are we really going to go over that again?" she asked with a sigh. How had she known the conversation would turn out this way? Easy. Because the only thing her mother and Lucy had in common was their mutual dislike of each other. And Shy always ended up getting caught in the middle.

"Why can't you date a woman who's more suitable for you? Someone who wants to make something of herself instead of leeching off other people?"

"I did."

"When?"

"Remember Heather, the basketball player I met when I was working at the sporting goods store in the mall? She's in the WNBA now. If you and Uncle Cristiano hadn't insisted I stop seeing her, you could have had a professional athlete for a daughter-in-law."

"You and her, you never would have worked out."

"Why? Because she was white?"

"No," her mother said much too quickly. "Because the two of you had too many differences. It's easier being with someone you don't have to explain things to. Someone who speaks your language and has shared the same experiences you have. You and Heather didn't have anything in common."

"Is that you talking or Uncle Cristiano? Because your argument sounds like one he would make."

"He's my brother. We have the same values. The values your father and I tried to instill in you. Love of family, pride in your community, and self-respect. Be friends with Lucy, but don't give your heart to her, honey. She may be one of us, but she doesn't deserve you. One day, you'll meet a woman—a nice Portuguese woman—who will."

Shy thought about Jake. Jake was honest, hard-working, and noble. Everything her mother said she wanted her to find in a partner. Everything except one.

"I've got to go, Mom. Lucy's train will be here soon."

"Have fun," her mother said with forced cheer. "Just not too much."

The comment was probably supposed to lighten the mood, but Shy didn't feel like laughing. She peered out the train station windows, her anxiety growing by the second. She had been looking forward to Lucy's visit for months. Now that the moment was almost here, she wasn't sure how she was supposed to feel. She was happy to have a taste of home, but what if it turned out to be bittersweet? And what if the feelings she had always had for Lucy were gone now? Eroded by time and distance, the old ties replaced by the bond she was developing with Jake.

"Jake is off-limits," she reminded herself. If she repeated the mantra often enough, maybe she'd start to believe it.

She popped out of her seat when she spotted a train approaching in the distance. The brakes squealed as the train gradually slowed and finally came to a stop. A few minutes later, the train doors opened, and uniformed porters disembarked. Passengers carrying briefcases, overnight bags, and more cumbersome luggage soon followed.

Shy craned her neck to get a better look. She saw weary businesspeople heading home after a long day's work and city dwellers anxious for a relaxing weekend getaway, but she didn't see Lucy. She was about to give up hope when she saw Lucy's familiar face bringing up the rear, her shoulder-length brown hair blowing in the breeze.

Lucy, an oversized black trash bag tossed over her shoulder, walked with one hand shoved deep into the pocket of her jeans. Her worn leather jacket was unzipped, revealing a faded T-shirt with an oversized picture of her favorite rapper's face emblazoned on the front. Her shoulders were drawn up around her ears as if she needed protection from the elements or the unfamiliar surroundings. Her dark brown eyes darted back and forth, taking in everything and everyone around her. Her gait was cautious; her expression, wary.

Shy watched her come, all tough girl attitude and Southie bravado. Shy thought she had never looked more beautiful. She smiled as she felt a familiar stirring low in her belly. The old fire was still burning after all.

Lucy paused as she walked into the waiting room. Shy raised a hand to get her attention. Lucy looked past the happy reunions going on all around her and broke into a grin. She lifted her chin to acknowledge Shy's greeting and began to walk toward her. Shy met her halfway.

"What's up, girl?" Lucy asked, giving her a one-armed hug.

"Same old, same old."

"Talk about a sight for sore eyes." Lucy took a step back and gave Shy's shoulder a squeeze as if she couldn't believe she was real. Shy knew the feeling. "You look good." Lucy let her hand drop as she looked her up and down. "Real good."

"So do you." Shy held out the bouquet of flowers, but Lucy didn't take it.

Lucy looked around to see who might be watching. "What's up with those?" she asked with a self-conscious laugh. "Are you on your way to the cemetery or the prom?"

"Neither one. I thought you'd like them, that's all."

"They're pretty and all, but you know that kind of thing ain't my style. You should have saved your money and given me the cash instead. I could have bought a new mix tape or some fresh new gear. Something that would last longer than a bunch of flowers."

Shy looked at the bouquet in her hand. She had asked the florist to give her wildflowers because she thought the blooms matched Lucy's untamed spirit. Now the gesture seemed as out of place as she had felt the day she'd stood on the dock hoping someone she had never met would give her a job. She walked over to the ticket window and handed the flowers to the clerk who had waited on her when she bought Lucy's train tickets.

"These are for you. Thanks for your help last week."

The clerk clutched the bouquet as if it was the first one she had ever received. "You're welcome."

Shy turned back to Lucy. "Are you ready to go?" she asked as she fished the keys to Jake's truck out of her pocket.

Lucy looked dubious. "Since when do you have wheels?"

"My boss let me borrow her truck for the weekend."

"She trusts you like that?"

Lucy sounded impressed, which made Shy feel important. Until they got outside and Lucy took a good look at the truck.

"No wonder she let you borrow it. The thing's a piece of shit. There's not much you can do to it that hasn't already been done."

Shy tried to see the truck through Lucy's eyes but couldn't. Yes, the battered pickup had its fair share of scratches and scrapes, but Shy thought the imperfections added character. Like an old pair of jeans that grew more frayed with each washing but fit better and better each time you pulled them on. When she looked at the truck, she didn't see the dents from a fender bender or the need for an overdue paint job. She saw Jake. Flawed but perfect in her own way.

"Fine." Shy twirled the key ring on her finger. "You can walk if you want. I'll ask Tess to save a spot for you at the bar. Right between two guys who have been out to sea on a swordfish boat for a month."

Shy climbed in the driver's seat and smiled to herself as Lucy jogged around to the passenger side.

"Wait. Hold up." Lucy tossed her bag in the floorboard and slammed the door shut. "You didn't say anything about a bar. Do they play good music?"

"A woman sings and plays guitar during Happy Hour. I like her. She's got a nice voice and her songs are really cool, but her second set usually ends at eight so we won't get to hear much of it. A DJ takes over when she finishes if you want to dance."

Whenever they went out, the only time Lucy left the dance floor was when the music slowed down. And that was the only time Shy wanted to be on it. Holding someone close and moving slow while the song's lyrics expressed all the feelings she couldn't put into words.

"That depends," Lucy said.

"On what?"

"If there are any cute guys in this town that don't smell like fish."

"Good luck with that."

"With what? Finding cute guys in a town this small or finding ones that don't smell like fish?"

"Both."

Lucy laughed. "Like you'd know. When was the last time you thought a guy was cute?"

"I can think it all day, but that doesn't mean I want to do anything about it."

"Do you seriously expect me to believe if Brad Pitt walked up to you right now and asked you to give it up, you'd say no?"

"Yes, I would. But if Angelina Jolie was doing the asking, it would be a different story."

"I feel you." Lucy held out her hand and slipped Shy some skin, rubbing away the momentary friction that had developed between them back at the train station. "I didn't mean for you to give your flowers away. I just wasn't expecting you to do something like that. You know I don't like people knowing my business."

"Yeah, I know. But no one knows you here. What does it matter if someone sees me giving you flowers?"

"It matters to me." Lucy stabbed the air with her hand as she tried to get her point across. A point Shy couldn't seem to understand, no matter how many times Lucy tried to explain it to her. "I don't want people thinking stuff about me that isn't true. I like being with you, Shy, but I'm not *like* you, you know what I mean?"

Shy told herself to let it go—to let the moment pass so she and Lucy wouldn't start the weekend with an argument—but she couldn't. She was tired of listening to Lucy's excuses about why they couldn't be together. She was ready to list the reasons they could. "Actually, no, I don't know what you mean."

Lucy's expression darkened. "What are you saying?"

Shy pulled into the parking lot of the Watering Hole, circled until she found an empty space, and shut off the truck's engine. "I'm saying I know how it feels when we're together. I know how I make *you* feel. It shouldn't matter what anyone else thinks as long as we're happy."

Lucy leaned against the door, putting much more than physical distance between them. "Why do you keep acting like we're girlfriends or something? I told you, Shy. We're friends. That's it."

"Friends with benefits, maybe," Shy said under her breath.

"I like guys," Lucy said as if she hadn't heard. "The only girl I fool around with is you. That doesn't make me gay. It doesn't make me bi. It just makes me who I am. I don't need a label, so stop trying to stick one on me."

"Fine. I won't ask you to define who or what we are as long as you tell me one thing. Why did you come to see me if you didn't want to be with me?"

Lucy took a long time to answer. As if she didn't know what to say or how to say it. When she finally spoke, though, everything she said was just right.

"Because Southie's not the same without you there. I missed you, girl. That's what I'm doing here." Lucy slid her hand across the seat, took Shy's hand in hers, and gave it a squeeze. "Now are you going to dance with me or what?"

Lucy got out of the truck without waiting for an answer and charged toward the Watering Hole. Shy caught up with her just inside the front door.

"I thought you said this place was cool," Lucy said in a voice that carried just a bit too far. Even Beverly McFarland, the singer who graced the stage for two separate hour-long sets each day, seemed to take notice. She frowned as she strummed her way to the end of a Gordon Lightfoot song. "There's hardly anyone here."

In truth, Shy had never seen the place so packed. The crowds Jake had said would be in town for Sunday's festivities must have shown up early because there wasn't a booth, table, or place at the bar to be had.

"I don't like it here," Lucy said after Beverly's set ended. Shy couldn't tell if she was talking about the bar or the town itself. "It's too quiet."

"In the beginning, I thought so, too. I had a really bad first few nights trying to get used to it, but now I love it. The quiet gives me a chance to think."

"That's why I don't like it," Lucy said. "I need lots of noise to drown out the voices in my head."

Hearing Lucy admit to occasionally feeling vulnerable made Shy feel closer to her. She liked it when Lucy let down her guard and offered her a rare peek inside her soul. Lucy had developed a thick protective shell around herself years ago to guard against the heartaches endemic to South Boston. A shell Shy had never been able to form but had always longed to have so she wouldn't cry herself to sleep each time someone broke her heart.

"This place does have one thing going for it, though," Lucy said as her eyes scanned the crowd.

"Yeah? What?"

"Him."

Lucy jerked her chin toward the bar. Shy looked toward the vague direction Lucy had indicated to see who she found so fascinating. Zach Anderson was standing near the bar, a trio of girls forming a semi-circle around him. Zach said something that made the girls laugh and twirl their hair flirtatiously. Then he looked up and waved.

"You know him?" Lucy asked after Shy waved back.

"He used to work on the *Mary Margaret*, but he's taking this season off."

"That's your boss's brother-in-law? I thought you said he was strung out. That guy might hit the occasional joint or pop some X now and then, but he's too hot to be a meth-head."

"That isn't Charlie. That's Zach. I told you about him, remember?"

"Oh, yeah. The college boy who defended you against the big, bad wolves. He's studying biology or something, right?"

"Botany."

Lucy waved her hand dismissively. "Same difference."

"Plants. Animals. Yeah, I can see how easily you could mix those up."

Lucy rolled her eyes. "Stop busting my balls before I take back what I said about missing you, shithead."

Hearing the familiar, if unusual, term of endearment made Shy smile with relief. Their circumstances might have changed, but their relationship was still the same. *She* was still the same.

"Are you going to introduce me to him or do I have to do it myself?" Lucy asked.

"Follow me."

Shy tried to clear a path through the crowd without spilling anyone's drinks along the way. Zach saw her coming and forged a path of his own.

"How are things on the boat?" he asked after he greeted her with a handshake. "Jake isn't talking your ear off, is she?"

"You know how she is. Just blah blah blah all the time." She and Zach laughed at the private joke. Lucy looked lost, so Shy whispered she would explain it to her later. "How are things up in Orono?"

"Awesome," Zach said. "I'm learning something new every day."

"Me, too."

"Yeah," he said with a nod. "Jake's one of the best teachers I've ever had. In school or out. She taught me everything I know about lobster fishing and a few things about life, too."

Lucy elbowed Shy in the ribs in a not-so-subtle effort to get her attention. Zach took a sip of his beer to hide his smile.

"Zach Anderson, this is Lucy Pereira, a friend of mine from Boston. Lucy, Zach."

Zach held out his hand. "Pleased to meet you, Lucy."

"You, too. Are you going to hang around for a while? If you are, I'll save a dance for you once the real music starts and I won't even make you buy me more than one, maybe two drinks in the meantime."

Zach looked at Shy as if he was asking her if it was okay for him and Lucy to be having this conversation. Shy was glad to see he appreciated relationship boundaries even if Lucy seemed to have no idea what they were. She nodded to show him it was okay. Until she met Jake and the rest of the people in this town, she had no idea so much could be said without even saying a word.

"That's a really tempting offer," Zach said, turning back to Lucy, "but I'll be leaving in a few minutes. I'm waiting for some friends to arrive. We're going to hit a couple more places after we leave here. I'm not much of a dancer, but I will buy you one, maybe two drinks while we wait. What'll you have?"

"A Bud Light."

"For you, Shy?"

Shy pointed to the Allagash in his hand. "Same as you."

Zach grinned. "Jake's influence has rubbed off on you, too, huh? I'll be right back."

Zach slowly made his way to the bar to order a round of drinks. While they waited, Lucy turned to Shy and looked at her hard.

"What?" Shy asked, wilting under the intense scrutiny.

"You've changed."

Shy felt a prickle of apprehension. Fitting in, not standing out, had always been her goal.

"How have I changed?"

"The Shy I know doesn't talk to guys in bars or have conversations that last longer than two seconds and she sure as hell doesn't drink some off-brand beer that probably tastes like ass." Lucy grabbed Shy by the shoulders and gave her a shake. "Who are you and what have you done with my friend?" she said, overacting like the heavily made-up star of a *telenovela*.

Shy knew she wasn't the same person she was when she'd arrived in Portland, but she didn't know how to explain the changes taking place inside her. "I'm still me," she said. "I'm just more me than I used to be."

"Whatever, dude." Lucy cursed under her breath. "Shit. I knew he was too good to be true."

At the bar, Zach greeted three new arrivals with kisses and warm hugs. The three new arrivals were men.

"Have a good evening, ladies," Zach said after he delivered their beers. "Perhaps I'll see you later?"

"Maybe," Shy said noncommittally. She had hoped she and Lucy would go back to her place when they left the Watering Hole, but after Zach's rejection, Lucy might want to go bar-hopping to find another prospect. "But Sunday at the festival for sure."

"Cool. The next round's on you," Zach said as he threw an arm around one of his friends' shoulders.

"You could have told me he was gay," Lucy said after Zach left.

"I might have if I'd known, but I thought you didn't like labels. Or is it only when they're applied to you?"

Lucy looked at her out of the corner of her eye. "Your boss is gay, too, right?"

"So is the woman who owns this place. Her partner is Jake's cousin. She owns the company Jake and I work for."

"No wonder you like it up here. You've found your people. Just don't forget the ones you left back in Southie. We're your people, too."

"I could never forget where I came from," Shy said defensively.

"It's not where you came from that worries me." Lucy took a long swallow of her beer as if she needed liquid courage to say what was on her mind. "It's where you're going."

"Where am I going?"

"Further away from me."

Shy heard genuine emotion in Lucy's voice. A mixture of longing, fear, and something Shy couldn't identify. It almost sounded like envy. Where they came from, people were so desperate to fit in with their predominantly Irish neighbors, they did everything they could not to stick out. In Portland, things were different. Being an individual was not only expected but celebrated.

"Portland's not that far from Boston," she said. "It's just a little over two hours by train."

"I'm not talking about the distance. I can handle that."

"Then what are you talking about?"

"Just like I said. You've changed, Shy, and I don't know if I like it."

For the longest time, Lucy's opinion of her was the only one that mattered. Shy didn't care if anyone else approved of her as long as Lucy did. Even though she was an adult now, she still wanted Lucy's approval—she probably always would—but earning it didn't seem as easy as it once had.

Why did growing up always mean growing apart?

Jake was planing wood for the spar of her boat when she heard a tentative knock on the shed door. For a brief, insane moment, she thought she'd open the door to find Susan standing on the other side.

Jake and her ex-lover hadn't spoken in nearly a year, and it had been even longer since they'd seen each other, but Rita had told her today that Susan would be in town for the festival and was hoping they could get together. At the time, Jake had written it off as Rita's attempt to play matchmaker. If Susan wanted to see her, she would have said so herself, and chances were it wouldn't happen at three in the morning. Then the knock came and Jake realized she wasn't quite so sure. About anything.

She pulled off her safety glasses, tossed them on her workbench, and opened the shed door. The glow from the fluorescent light overhead fell on the faces of Shy and a young woman who was as equally striking as Shy but whose beauty had a harder edge. Jake didn't know whether to feel disappointed or relieved.

"When I rang the bell at the house and didn't get an answer, I knew I'd find you in here," Shy said brightly. "I'm not disturbing you, am I? I wanted to introduce you to someone." She beckoned for her companion to move forward.

Jake wiped her hand on her jeans to make sure no wood shavings were stuck to her palm. "You must be Lucy."

"A pleasure." Lucy shook Jake's hand limply as she directed a question toward Shy. "What did you tell her about me?"

Shy looked stricken by the question so Jake answered for her.

"Just that she was looking forward to your visit and couldn't wait to spend time with you. Did you two have fun tonight?" she asked as she tried to get a handle on the vibe between them.

Shy and Lucy shared a look as if one was pleading with the other to be tactful.

"Shy took me to the Watering Hole," Lucy said at length. "Tomorrow, we're supposed to do some sightseeing and have dinner at a place called DiMillo's."

Jake nodded appreciatively. DiMillo's was a sixty-year-old family-owned restaurant located near the marina. People came for the novelty of eating in a floating restaurant that offered incredible views of Portland Harbor. They stayed because DiMillo's served some of the freshest seafood on the waterfront. The food was good, but it wasn't cheap. Unless you went early enough to order one of the dinner specials, a meal for two could cost you three figures, easy.

Shy must really want to make a favorable impression, Jake thought. DiMillo's was the kind of place you went to celebrate a special occasion or make new memories you hoped would eventually be remembered as one. It was the place where she had once planned to ask Susan to marry her. But that was before the future they had planned became a thing of the past.

"Do you have any recommendations?" Shy asked.

"Try the DiMillo's Lobsterbake. You can get enough food for two people for less than fifty bucks."

Shy smiled. "I meant recommendations for sightseeing. I have a few places in mind, like Palace Playland, but what's something you think we shouldn't miss?"

Jake took off her hat and ran her hand through her hair to give herself time to think. If she were trying to impress Shy, she'd take her on an early morning hike on Back Cove Trail to watch the sun rise over the pines or on a leisurely boat ride to watch the sun set over the ocean. She didn't know Lucy as well as she was beginning to know Shy, though, so she had no idea if any of Maine's many natural wonders would appeal to her more than its man-made ones.

"There's always something to do in Old Port," she finally said, "but you're going to be there on Sunday for the festival. If you want to relax before the madness starts, you can go to Deering Oaks Park and feed the ducks, but it can get a little sketchy down there at night."

"I thought you said Portland was one of the safest cities in the country."

"It is, but everything's relative, right? Try Casco Bay or Peaks Island instead. You could rent bikes and explore the trails or spend the day wandering in and out of the shops."

"That sounds cool. Don't you think so, Luce? We can go to Palace Playland the next time you're in town."

"If you say so. We'll talk about it later. Right now, though, I'm ready to turn in." Lucy directed her words to Shy but looked at Jake as if she were warning her to stay away from her territory. "Let's go back to your place."

"Sure. Okay."

Shy snapped to attention as if she was used to doing Lucy's bidding, and Lucy led the way out of the shed as if she was certain Shy would follow.

"See you later, Jake."

Seeing the expectant look in Shy's eyes, Jake didn't have to work too hard to imagine what she and Lucy were about to do. She found herself wishing she could take Lucy's place. Kissing Shy. Touching her. Feeling Shy's body move against hers. She briefly closed her eyes to erase the images from her mind.

"Have a good night."

Shy closed the shed door behind her and jogged to catch up with Lucy. "What's your hurry?" she asked as they climbed the stairs to her apartment.

"I want to see where you live. You've never had a place of your own before. You've always been crammed in with your mother, your brothers, and your sister."

Shy unlocked the door and turned on the lights. "What do you think?"

Lucy dropped her bag on the floor and took a look around. "This is a sweet setup, Shy. And you've got it all to yourself? How much is Jake paying you?"

Shy didn't want to discuss her salary because she didn't want Lucy to think she was bragging. After she paid her bills, allotted herself a small allowance, and sent her mother some money to help around the house, she stashed the rest of her paycheck in a savings account that didn't earn much interest but paid more than any of the hiding places she used to use.

"She pays me enough."

"Obviously." Lucy ran her hand over the top of the small flat-screen TV. "I should move out of my dinky little apartment and bunk down here with you."

"Really? You'd do that?"

Lucy already had a roommate and they were on pretty good terms, so she and Shy had never talked about moving in together. Now that Lucy had brought it up, Shy couldn't get the idea out of her head. They could split the rent and the utilities and try to build the life Lucy kept trying to convince her they could never have.

"I'd do it in a heartbeat if I didn't think Jake might have something to say about it." Lucy walked over to the coffee table, picked up the miniature lobster boat, and turned it over in her hands. "Do the two of you have something going on or what?"

"Me and Jake? Why would you think that?" Shy thought she had kept her burgeoning feelings for Jake on the down low. She was shocked to discover Lucy might have picked up on them.

"When you call me, you can't stop talking about her. It's always 'Jake said this' and 'Jake said that' or 'Jake did this' and 'Jake did that.' You talk about her like she's your girlfriend. And she sure as hell looks at you like she's yours. She didn't seem too happy to see me when she opened the door a few minutes ago."

Shy had noticed the strange look on Jake's face when Jake had opened the shed door, but she had attributed it to Jake being unhappy about being disturbed, not jealous over seeing Shy with Lucy.

"That's crazy, Luce. You don't know what you're talking about."

Shy picked up Lucy's bag and took it to the bedroom, not expecting Lucy to follow. But when she turned around, Lucy was right there, pushing her down on the bed and covering her body with her own.

"Don't I? Why do you think I got you out of that shed so fast? So I could see your decorating skills? Hell, no. I got you out of there so I could do this."

Lucy dipped her head, caught Shy's lower lip between her teeth, and gave it a gentle tug. Shy didn't feel anything until she imagined Jake hovering above her. Then desire swept through her like a wildfire.

She moaned as Lucy ran the tip of her tongue across her lip and slowly drew it into her mouth. When Shy tried to deepen the kiss, Lucy pulled away, a teasing smile on her full lips.

"How long has it been?" she asked, pinning Shy's shoulders to the bed.

"Too long."

Shy blinked until the image of Jake went away and Lucy's face came into focus. She needed to concentrate on the woman in front of her, not the one she couldn't have.

She forced herself to keep her hands at her sides, even though she wanted nothing more than to bury them in Lucy's hair and pull her in for another kiss. A kiss to make her remember. A kiss to make her forget.

But this was Lucy's game, which meant playing by her rules. So Shy waited to see where the game would lead.

Lucy ground her hips against Shy's. Unable to keep still, Shy returned the pressure. Lucy kissed her again. Briefly. Like the appetizer before the main meal. Lucy didn't need to whet Shy's appetite. Shy was already starving.

"Do you want to?" Lucy asked after another of those teasing kisses. "Or are you too tired after working all day?"

"What do you think?"

Shy ran her hands over the rise of Lucy's hips and watched her eyes go dark the way they always did when Lucy was aroused. When she was about to come, her brown eyes turned almost black. Shy slipped a hand under Lucy's shirt and watched her eyes grow darker still.

"God, that feels good," Lucy said after Shy unhooked her bra and cupped her breasts in her hands, her fingers gently kneading the soft, warm flesh.

Lucy rolled off Shy and lay on her back, silently granting permission for Shy to continue what she had started. Shy pulled Lucy's T-shirt over her head and tossed her bra aside. Then she circled Lucy's navel with her tongue, smiling to herself when she heard Lucy's hiss of pleasure.

"Come on," Lucy said, pushing Shy's head lower. "Don't make me wait."

Shy unbuttoned Lucy's jeans and pulled them off. Her thong underwear joined the growing pile of clothes on the floor. Lucy bucked when Shy slowly dragged her tongue across her sex. Shy gripped her ass with both hands to hold her in place.

"Yeah, baby, just like that."

Being with Lucy was a negotiation. Like hashing out a peace treaty at the end of a war. Lucy could initiate the proceedings, but she couldn't finish. She could receive pleasure, but she couldn't give it. Shy didn't mind. Hearing Lucy's throaty cries, seeing her boneless and satisfied after one orgasm after another ripped through her body was enough. Usually. Tonight, Shy felt like something was missing.

"Where are you?" Lucy asked afterward as she threw a possessive leg over Shy's thigh and hooked her heel around her calf.

Shy tried to sound reassuring. "I'm right here."

"Then why does it feel like you're worlds away?" Lucy put a finger under Shy's chin and forced her to turn to face her. "Come back to me."

Shy kissed the tip of her nose. "I'm right here, Luce. I'm not going anywhere."

"Promise?"

"I promise."

Lucy closed her eyes and quickly fell asleep while Shy absently stroked her hair. Shy stared at the ceiling. As Lucy's shallow breathing grew deeper, she wondered if she had just made a promise she couldn't keep.

CHAPTER TWELVE

Shy secured her bicycle in the rack outside Micah's Bike Rentals and Repairs and poked her head inside the shop to let the owner know she and Lucy no longer needed the bikes they had selected.

"You haven't been gone that long." Micah, a dreadlocked hipster in hemp shorts and a Tour de France T-shirt, moved away from the ten-speed he was tinkering on to come outside and take a look at the mountain bikes Shy and Lucy had rented less than an hour ago. "Was there something wrong with the bikes?" he asked as he checked the chain, wheels, and brakes on the first cycle.

"No, everything was fine," Shy said. "We just changed our minds, that's all."

Micah wiped his hands on an oil-stained rag and brushed a twisted coil of dark blond hair out of his eyes. "Hold on. Let me issue you a partial refund for your trouble."

Shy shook her head. "Consider it a down payment for the next trip."

Micah stuck out his hand. "You've got a deal. See you next time."

"What now?" Lucy asked.

"I don't know. You tell me."

Shy had been looking forward to a fun-filled day spent outdoors, but she and Lucy had turned back from the trail after less than two miles. Lucy hadn't liked the fit of her bike, the steepness of the terrain, the time, the temperature, or pretty much anything to do with the outing Shy had planned.

"Cool. Let's go shopping. I don't think they sell anything but flannel in this town, but it doesn't hurt to look."

With a heavy sigh, Shy looked up at the bright blue sky overhead. The sky was clear and beautiful, but the day she had spent underneath it had been much cloudier. Lucy had been in a crappy mood all day. Shy felt partially responsible for Lucy's ill temper. She shouldn't have slept with Lucy when she wasn't fully in the moment. Lucy hadn't said anything about last night, but she knew Shy well enough to know something had been off.

"The place you're taking me to tonight," Lucy said as she pressed her face to the window of a clothing store. "Is it fancy?"

"DiMillo's? I don't know. I've never been there before."

"Then how did you find out about it?"

"Rita, a lady who works at my bank, told me it's the place to go when you want to have a really good sit-down meal."

"So it is fancy." Lucy looked down at her jeans and T-shirt and frowned in disapproval. "I need something to wear. This store looks promising, but I don't have the cash for a new outfit."

Shy bit her tongue. Lucy had been complaining about money—more specifically, her lack of it—since breakfast at Opal's Diner, when she'd conveniently gone missing after the waitress brought their check. She hadn't come right out and hit Shy up for cash, but she seemed to be working her way up to it. Shy didn't want money to become a wedge between them when they already had more than enough issues driving them apart.

"You don't have to buy anything new. We're the same size. You can borrow some of my clothes."

"Most of your wardrobe consists of hoodies, jeans, and work boots. You don't want me going out looking like a slob, do you?" Lucy ducked inside the store—the sign over the door read Sew and Sew—and began looking through the racks of clothes. "Besides, I thought you liked it when I dressed up for you."

"I do, but you could make anything look good, whether it cost five bucks or five hundred." Shy checked the price tag on a blouse that caught her eye. The items in the store were a lot closer to the high end of her price range than the low one. She placed the blouse back on the rack. Perhaps they should forget about going out to dinner and stay in and order pizza instead.

"But you like me best in nothing at all, don't you?"

Shy didn't respond. She felt guilty about last night. She had thought being with Lucy would help put Jake out of her mind. Instead, Jake was dominating her thoughts now more than ever. She had been thinking about her all day, wondering if she should have invited Jake on the bike ride instead of Lucy. Lucy's favorite physical activity was sex. She would have preferred staying in bed all day. At one time, Shy might have, too, but after last night, she knew those days were gone.

She owed Lucy an apology and an explanation, but she didn't know how to formulate either without having Lucy accuse her of betraying her roots. Where they came from, you were supposed to stick with your own, not turn your back on them. But if her heart was leading her down another path, how was she supposed to resist?

Lucy picked up a blouse and held it against her voluptuous body. "What do you think?"

The cream color perfectly complemented Lucy's skin and eyes. The low cut wouldn't leave much to the imagination, but that was typical Lucy. She loved putting her assets on display. Shy preferred to keep hers under wraps. The sweater she had worn to dinner at Jake's was as daring as she got. She had been tempted not to buy it for fear her friends back in Boston would say she was trying to be something she wasn't, but she had ignored those voices and chosen to listen to the one that said she could be anything she wanted to be. She needed that voice to lead her now, but it had fallen silent.

"I like it," she said. "It's pretty."

"Pretty isn't going to cut it. I want something that'll make people's eyes bug out of their heads. Something like this."

Lucy put the blouse back and reached for another. And another. And another. Several things caught her eye, but nothing seemed to fit her exacting standards. She had been selecting and dismissing items for several minutes when one of the sales clerks left her position behind the register and stationed herself next to the clearance rack a few feet away. Even though she appeared to be straightening the clothes, Shy could tell she was more interested in her and Lucy. Every time they moved, so did she. Whenever Shy looked up, the clerk was watching. But if Shy tried to make eye contact, the woman would quickly turn away.

"Here we go," Lucy said under her breath. "I'll bet she doesn't get too many of us in here. She probably thinks we're trying to steal something."

Shy felt something shift inside. She was tired of being followed in stores or avoided on the street because she looked a certain way. It happened all the time at home, but until now, it hadn't happened in Portland. Shy had thought things were different here. It saddened her to realize people's prejudices didn't change even if her location did.

"May I help you with something?" she asked angrily after the woman continued to follow her and Lucy around the store.

The clerk put down the sweater she had been pretending to fold and moved closer. "I don't mean to bother you, but I couldn't help noticing you when you came in."

"Yeah? And?"

"Aren't you the greenhorn working on Jake Myers' boat this season? The one who took Charlie's place?"

"Yes," Shy said warily, not quite sure where the conversation was going. Was the woman a friend of Jake's or of Charlie's? If she was on Charlie's side, the afternoon might be about to take an even more unpleasant turn.

"My name's Eleanor Parker. I own this shop. My daughter, India, is a big fan of fishing in general and the *Mary Margaret* in particular. It isn't often we see one woman operating a lobster boat, let alone two. India says she wants to be just like you and

Jake when she grows up." She pumped Shy's hand in both of hers. "I wanted to thank you for being such a good role model."

That was something Shy didn't hear every day. She felt like kicking herself for assuming the worst about someone who only wanted to wish her well. Prejudice, it seemed, worked both ways.

"How old is your daughter?"

"She just turned nine."

"So my job's safe for at least a few years."

"I don't know," Eleanor said with a proud smile. "India's pretty precocious. If she had her way, she'd give you a run for your money sooner than you might think."

"I'll make sure to watch my back."

Eleanor turned from Shy to Lucy. "Are you finding anything you like?"

"Plenty," Lucy said, "but nothing I can afford." She placed the blouse she was holding back on the rack where she had found it. "Come on, Shy."

Lucy pushed the swinging door open and headed outside.

"It was nice meeting you, Eleanor," Shy said, then hurried to catch up to Lucy. "Do you want to keep shopping, or would you rather go home? If you want to go back to my place, there's a six-pack of Bud Light in the fridge with your name on it."

"Your place," Lucy said sarcastically. "Your place is in Boston, Shy, not here. You're acting like you belong here, but this isn't home. No matter what that lady said, you're just a visitor here. Same as me. Enjoy it while you can, but you can't stay here forever. You've got to come home sometime."

Shy was beginning to wonder where home was. Was it back in Southie or was it here?

Home, she had once heard was where the heart was. Unfortunately, her heart didn't know where to turn.

❖

Jake muted the sound on the telecast of the Red Sox-Blue Jays game when she heard her doorbell ring. She placed the remote on the coffee table and pushed herself off the couch. She wasn't expecting company, so she peered through the peephole to see who was standing on her front porch. One of Bruce Thornton's grandkids, a box of pizza in his hands, reached for the doorbell again and leaned against it long enough to wake the dead.

"Evening, Chad," Jake said after she opened the door.

"Evening, Jake." Chad removed his ear buds and let them dangle down the front of his tomato-red Nonna's Pizza polo shirt. Tinny heavy metal music blasted from the miniature speakers as he referred to the slip of paper taped to the top of the pizza box, then lifted his visor to scratch his buzz-cut head.

Jake leaned against the doorjamb as Chad screwed up his face in concentration just like his grandfather did when he was hunting for swordfish. "Is there a problem?"

"Ayuh, I think there might be." Chad reached for the MP3 player clipped to the waistband of his sagging uniform pants and flipped the power switch. The music came to an abrupt stop right in the middle of the lead singer's ear-splitting wail. "I've got a delivery, but the name doesn't match the address. You don't have an Ashley Silva living here, do you?"

"That's my greenhorn. She lives in the apartment over the garage. But I doubt she ordered pizza. The last I heard, she was planning on going out for dinner tonight."

"That's not what this says." Chad plucked the scrap of paper off the box and turned it around so she could see it. "One large ultimate with extra cheese to be delivered to this address."

"Fine. I'll pay you so you can finish the rest of your deliveries and I'll figure it out later." Jake dug some cash out of her pocket. "What's the damage?"

"Twelve bucks."

Jake counted out a five and a ten. "Here's fifteen. Keep the change."

"Thanks, Jake."

Chad put his ear buds back in and bounded down the stairs, his arms thrashing wildly to the rhythm of the music from his private concert.

Jake climbed the stairs behind the garage and knocked on the door. Shy opened the door and stepped onto the landing, her eyes downcast as she sorted through the bills in her hand.

"How much do I owe you?" Shy asked without looking up.

"Fifteen bucks, including the tip."

"Jake?" Shy snapped her head up, her eyes wide. "What are you doing here?"

Jake indicated the cardboard box in her hands. "The pizza guy delivered to the wrong house."

"Trade you."

"I thought you were going out tonight," Jake said after she exchanged the pizza for cash.

Shy looked over her shoulder and reached behind her to pull the door shut. "We were supposed to, but…"

Shy's voice trailed off, but she didn't need to finish her sentence for Jake to gather her meaning. Lucy's visit obviously wasn't going as well as Shy had hoped.

Shy carefully balanced the pizza box on the railing so it wouldn't tip over and fall to the ground ten feet below. "Can I ask you something?" she asked as she traced the red and green lettering on the pizza box with her fingertip.

"Sure. What's on your mind?"

"I know you haven't known me that long, but do I seem… different to you?"

"In what way?"

"Lucy says I've changed. She makes it sound like a bad thing."

"When someone says you've changed, it usually means you've stopped living your life their way." Jake ducked her head to force Shy to look her in the eye. She wanted to be sure Shy heard what she was about to say. "It doesn't matter what anyone else thinks about you, Shy. What matters is what you think about you. You've grown both as a person and an employee in the short time I've known you. Those are accomplishments that should be celebrated instead of belittled."

"Thanks. That's good to hear. Can I ask you something else?"

"You'd better make it quick. Your pizza's getting cold."

"Why did you and Susan break up? Was it sudden or did you grow apart gradually over time?"

Jake couldn't remember Shy asking her something so personal. Like most questions, it said more about the mindset of the person doing the asking than the one tasked with providing an answer. Shy's normally bright eyes were clouded with sadness as she waited to hear an answer she would most likely apply to the questions running through her own mind. Jake folded her arms in front of her chest and leaned against the railing, being careful not to dislodge the pizza.

"It happened—"

"Well, if it isn't Captain Jake." Lucy opened the door and joined them on the landing. The tip of the joint in her left hand glowed bright orange as she brought it to her lips and inhaled deeply. "Want a hit?" she asked after she blew out a thick stream of smoke.

"No, thank you." Jake backed away from the proffered joint and settled her gaze on Shy. "I thought we had an agreement." She tried to control her emotions, but she couldn't rein them in. Her voice shook with barely controlled anger. "I let Charlie go because he couldn't control his drug use. I took a chance on you with the understanding you wouldn't partake in recreational drugs during the season. I'm disappointed in you, Shy."

"But I didn't do—"

Jake held up her hands. "No excuses. I'm going to make an appointment with Dr. Halloran's office. You're taking a urine test first thing Monday morning. If it comes back dirty, you're fired. In the meantime, you're suspended until the results come in. I can't have you on my boat unless and until I know you're clean."

"I understand, but, Jake—"

"Save your breath. We'll talk after the results come in."

Jake stomped down the stairs, choosing to swallow her disappointment rather than give voice to it. If she did, her neighbors would be calling the cops on her for disturbing the peace. She didn't know which was worse, the fact that Shy had let her down or the gleeful look on her so-called friend's face as Lucy reveled in her fall.

"Lighten up," Lucy said to Jake's departing form. "It was only one joint."

To emphasize her point, she flicked the remains of the doobie off the landing. It slowly tumbled through the air, its still-lit orange end lighting up the darkening sky, before it landed at Jake's feet. The ground was too wet from the daily rain showers for the grass to catch fire, but Jake ground the joint under the heel of her boot to make sure. She picked up the crushed joint with a glare that spoke volumes, but didn't say anything as she walked away.

"Cut it out, Lucy." Shy grabbed her by the arm and pulled her inside.

"Wait. Don't forget the pizza." Lucy broke free and grabbed the box off the railing. After she kicked the door shut with her foot, she dropped the pizza box on the coffee table, opened the lid, and helped herself to a slice. "This is pretty good. You want some?"

Shy was too upset to even think about food. She had received dressing-downs before, but Jake's stinging rebuke had hurt more than the others. And the sad part was it didn't even have to happen if Jake had believed in her as much as she claimed to.

"Why would you pull a stunt like that, Luce? Are you trying to get me fired?"

"It was one joint. And you weren't even smoking. I was. I didn't think she'd take it so seriously."

"Bullshit. Why do you think I asked you not to bring your stash with you in the first place?"

"I didn't bring it. I bought this after I got here," Lucy said as if that made all the difference. "While you were talking to some of your 'friends' at the bar last night, I got the hook-up from a guy in the parking lot. It's good stuff, too. You should try some. It might help you relax. Last night definitely didn't do the trick."

Lucy pulled a plastic bag filled with loosely rolled joints out of her jacket pocket and tossed it on the coffee table. Shy grabbed the bag and headed to the bathroom.

"What are you doing?" Lucy asked as she reached for another slice of pizza.

"What do you think I'm doing?" Shy opened the baggie and crumbled the joints into the toilet bowl.

"Don't." Lucy dropped the pizza in the box, scrambled off the couch, and ran to the bathroom. "I paid good money for those."

"I hope it was money well spent." Shy blocked Lucy's desperate grab for the now-empty bag and flushed the toilet. She watched the weed and rolling papers circle the bowl, then disappear down the drain.

"Since when did you turn into such a narc?" Lucy followed her into the bedroom. "What are you doing now?"

Shy opened the drawer she had set aside for Lucy, removed the clothes inside, and shoved them into the trash bag that served as Lucy's suitcase. "Packing your things."

"But it's Saturday night. My train doesn't leave until Monday morning."

"The train might be leaving Monday, but you're leaving to-night." Shy tossed her the trash bag. "I'm taking you home myself."

"Seriously, Shy." Lucy rolled her eyes. "I remember when you used to be able to take a joke. This is about Jake, isn't it? You're not pissed at me for what I did. You're pissed at her for being so quick to assume you were doing it, too."

Shy looked away to hide the hurt she knew must be evident on her face. She swiped at her eyes, which stung from unshed tears.

"See?" Lucy said. "I knew the two of you had something going on. Don't be mad at me because your Anglo doesn't have faith in you. She's known you only a few months. I've known you all your life." She kneaded the tense muscles in the back of Shy's neck. "She could never understand you like I do. In your heart, you know what I'm saying is true."

Lucy's voice was as soothing as the rhythm of her fingers.

"You've lost jobs before. What's one more? Once you get back to Boston and leave these hicks behind, you'll realize I did you a favor tonight. Get your things. Let's pack our shit and blow this town for good."

It would be so easy to do what Lucy suggested. To turn tail and run. But Shy chose to do the right thing, not the easy thing. She chose to stand her ground.

"I can't go."

"But you don't have any reason to stay."

"I have every reason. I'm not going anywhere until I clear my name."

"And then what? Don't tell me you intend to stay here after what went down tonight."

"I came here to do a job and I'm not leaving until it's done."

Lucy looked at her, her eyes filled with disappointment. "Are you still willing to say you don't think you've changed?" She cupped Shy's cheek in the palm of her hand. "You said you were going to come back to me, but that was a lie, wasn't it? I've already lost you for good, haven't I?"

"Luce—"

Lucy pressed her fingers against Shy's lips. "Don't say anything. The only thing left to say is good-bye."

Shy couldn't bring herself to say the word. How could she say good-bye to the best friend she had ever had? She remembered all the laughs they had shared and the fun times they'd had over the years. Whenever something good happened to her, Lucy had always been the first person she wanted to share the news with. Whenever something bad happened, Lucy was the person she had sought out to make her feel better. There were some things her family wouldn't understand and some things they didn't need to hear. Who was she supposed to talk to if she didn't have Lucy to turn to?

"I love you, Luce."

Shy drew Lucy into her arms and gave her a hug. She knew she and Lucy would never be lovers again, but maybe one day they could go back to being friends.

"I love you, too, shithead." Lucy let go and gathered her things. "Now take me home."

Traffic on the interstate was relatively smooth, but the drive to Boston seemed to take a lot longer than two hours. When Shy pulled to a stop in front of Lucy's apartment building, she expected Lucy to lay into her one last time. To release the emotions she had kept bottled up during the much-too-quiet drive from Portland. Instead, Lucy remained uncharacteristically somber.

"You have feelings for Jake, don't you?"

Shy nodded, too tired to deny it.

"Your uncle's going to have a cow when he finds out."

"Tell me something I don't know."

"What are you going to tell your mom?"

Shy slid down in the driver's seat. "I haven't figured it out yet."

"Good luck with that," Lucy said with a teasing smile. Then her smile slowly faded and her eyes misted. "Good luck with everything."

Before Shy could say anything in response, Lucy bolted from the truck. Shy watched her until she was safely inside the building, then she put the truck in gear and headed home. She needed to tell her mother about her budding feelings for Jake in case Lucy said something, either accidentally or intentionally, while she wasn't around to tell the whole story.

Her mother's face fell as soon as she opened the door. "You got fired, didn't you?"

"No, I brought Lucy home early and decided to come see everyone before I headed back to Portland."

Her mother looked skeptical. "Are you sure?"

"Yes, I'm sure." Shy dropped the packages in her hands so she could hug Laura and Danny. She tried to hug Federico, too, but he pushed her away.

"Stop. I'm too old for that mushy stuff."

"Are you too old for these, too?" Shy held out the box of designer tennis shoes she had bought him for his birthday. "If you are, I can take them back to the Nike store and ask for a refund."

Federico snatched the box out of her hands to make sure she didn't follow through on her threat.

"What do you say?" her mother asked.

"Thanks, Shy." Federico gave her a quick hug.

"Happy early birthday, buddy."

She kissed him on the top of his head and watched fondly as he kicked off his old shoes and plopped down on the floor to try on his new ones. Then he, Laura, and Danny treated her to an impromptu fashion show as they paraded around the living room wearing the new gear she had bought them. After the show was over, her mother drew her into the kitchen so they could talk in private.

"Thank you for making everyone so happy. Now tell me why you're really here."

Shy wanted to tell her everything—to tell her about her feelings for Jake—but the words got stuck in her throat. "I didn't get fired," she said, trying to ease the worry she saw etched on her mother's face, "but I am suspended until I pass a drug test."

"Oh, Shy." Her mother threw her hands into the air. "Didn't I tell you this would happen if you spent time with Lucy Pereira?"

"Yes, but I didn't do anything wrong this time."

"According to you, you never do. But in my book, guilty by association is still guilty. Jake's family has been good to ours," her mother said earnestly. "Cristiano says they're good people. If he says it's so, I can't help but believe him. Do whatever you have to do to make her forgive you. Apologize for what you did and pray she'll take you back."

Shy was unable to hide her frustration at having to defend herself against someone else's actions. "Didn't you hear what I said? *I* didn't do anything wrong. It was Lucy who—"

"You chose to invite Lucy up there, which means you're responsible for her actions as well as yours. Take responsibility, Ashley. You can't point fingers at other people every time something goes wrong."

Shy was too tired to argue.

Evidently feeling she had finally gotten her point across, her mother let up on the onslaught and patted her hand. "Do you like Jake? Is she a good boss?"

"She's—"

Smart, sexy, and brave. A total badass and the most incredible woman I've ever met. I haven't even kissed her yet, but I think I might be falling in love with her.

Shy looked into her mother's eyes, which finally gazed at her with the approval she had sought for so long, and she couldn't bring herself to say the words she had longed to say.

"Like Uncle Cristiano said, she's good people."

CHAPTER THIRTEEN

Jake's anger gave way to concern after she peered through the living room window and noticed Shy still hadn't returned with her truck. She wasn't worried about the pickup. That's what insurance was for. She was worried about Shy. More specifically, her state of mind when she'd driven away three hours ago.

Where was she and what was she up to? She had looked hurt and angry when Jake confronted her about her possible drug use. Was she blowing off steam now or doing something self-destructive?

Jake ran her hands through her hair and fought to keep from pulling it out by the roots. The uncertainty was killing her.

She turned away from the window but quickly turned back when a vehicle pulled into the driveway. The vehicle wasn't her truck, but a car she found just as familiar. Her visitor climbed out of the SUV and walked across the lawn with a slight hitch in her step. She reached for the railing as she climbed the front steps. Jake opened the door before she could ring the bell.

"I thought it might be too late to drop by, then I remembered Mom telling me you keep some rather strange hours these days. I'm surprised I didn't find you in your woodshed. Or aren't you working on a boat at the moment?"

Jake was so flustered she didn't know what to say. So she started with the obvious.

"Susan."

Susan opened her arms for a hug and Jake reluctantly walked into them, feeling out of place in what had once been her second home.

"You seem surprised to see me," Susan said. "Didn't Mom tell you I was in town?"

"Yes, but I'm surprised to see you here. Is Mallory with you?"

"She wanted to come, but she couldn't make it. She's on call this weekend and has to be available in case of emergencies. She sends her regards, though."

"Sure she does."

Mallory Walters was the surgeon who had performed four of the six procedures on Susan's left leg after it was mangled by debris from one of the two pipe bombs set near the finish line of the Boston Marathon.

Jake had watched Susan and Mallory grow closer during Susan's extended hospital stay. And after she brought Susan home to heal, she had eventually watched her walk away to be with Mallory. Someone who only knew her as she was now— an amputee with a prosthetic left leg—instead of the person she was before April 15, 2013, the last Patriots' Day Jake would ever celebrate with a clear conscience.

Stopping by the marathon to watch runners stream across the finish line had been Jake's idea. Knowing what had happened at eleven minutes to three wasn't her fault didn't make her feel less responsible. Susan called it survivor's guilt. Jake preferred to call it empathizing for someone she loved. Someone who used to love her in return.

"What brings you here?" Jake asked after they settled in the living room. Her heart ached at the hauntingly familiar sight of Susan curled up in her favorite chair.

"I wanted to know how you've been. Mom tells me you've made some changes on the boat. Getting rid of Charlie was long overdue. How's the greenhorn working out for you?"

Jake felt the sharp sting of tonight's disappointment. "In a few days, I might be on the lookout for another one."

"What happened?"

"There was an incident earlier tonight. My greenhorn. Her name's Ashley Silva, but she prefers to be called Shy. She's renting the apartment over the garage. When I went up there tonight, I caught a friend of hers smoking pot. I don't know if Shy was smoking, too. I have to wait for the results of the urine test to find out. If the results say she lit up, she's out."

"Have you already scheduled the test?"

"Not yet. I'm hoping to set something up for Monday morning, which could cost me up to half a day of fishing. Unless the lab puts a rush on the results, I won't know anything until Wednesday or Thursday at the earliest."

"That's a long time to be without help. What are you going to do for four days without a greenhorn?"

"Either man the boat myself or see if I can talk Kate out of retirement. Going it alone is too dangerous—anything could happen on the open water—but Kate has other responsibilities now. I don't want to call on her if I don't have to."

"What about me? I've got the week off from work. I could pitch in."

Jake tried to keep from staring at Susan's prosthesis.

"When was the last time you went lobster fishing?" The answer was probably longer than Susan cared to admit, but Jake needed to know. If she took Susan up on her crazy idea, she wanted to be sure no one would get hurt. Her sanity depended on it.

"The year Kate showed you and me the ropes. But fishing's a bit like riding a bike, isn't it? Once you learn, you never forget how to do it. I think it would be fun. What do you say? We'd get to spend some time together and I'd get to show you I'm capable of more than you think I am."

When they were coming apart, Susan had accused Jake of smothering her after the accident. Of wanting to do everything for her instead of letting her try and fail. There might have been some truth to Susan's argument, but Jake had hated watching her growing frustration as she struggled to do all the things that had once come easy.

"All right," Jake said, seeing how much tackling this current challenge meant to Susan. "I'll pick you up at Rita's after I get back from Doc Halloran's office."

But she planned to keep Kate on standby just in case. She had no doubt Susan could do anything she set her mind to, but she thought the novelty of the grueling work would wear off after a few hours. Then she'd be down not one greenhorn but two.

Susan grinned, the flames from the fireplace showing off the highlights in her strawberry blond hair. "Mallory won't know what to think when I call to tell her the news."

"She'll probably think you're crazy."

Susan's grin grew even broader. "She already knows that."

Jake didn't need to ask if Susan and Mallory were happy. The glow on Susan's face told her everything she needed to know. Almost everything. Jake still didn't know why Susan had decided to pay a visit to the house they used to share. They couldn't change the past and they had no future. The present was all that remained and it, too, was uncertain.

"Are you going to the festival tomorrow?" Susan asked.

Jake stared at the flickering flames in the fireplace. "I don't do crowds. And I'm sure you understand why."

She looked up in time to see the memories of that day play out on Susan's face. The initial excitement, followed by confusion, anxiety, and fear. With a faraway look in her eyes, Susan hugged her knees to her chest and rubbed the spot where her stump fit into her prosthesis.

"That was a dark day for everyone who was there—and even the ones that weren't," Susan said. "The first night I came home, I remember freaking out over the fireworks after the Sea Dogs game, thinking the madness was happening all over again."

Jake had the same reaction even now. She circled the days the team planned to hold fireworks displays so she could prepare herself for the noise. She couldn't hear a loud percussive sound or see a seemingly abandoned backpack without assuming the worst and looking for a safe place to hide. The safest places she had found distanced her from the rest of the world—and, occasionally, from those she loved most. She hated missing milestones in their lives—Pete's no-hitter for the Sea Dogs, Morgan's twelfth birthday party at Palace Playland—but she didn't want them to be traumatized by her inevitable panic attack as the crowds pressed in on her and the unwanted notion took hold that they were being targeted once more.

Her family had tried to tell her she was being overly cautious. That she shouldn't put her life on hold to protect herself from something that might not come to pass. Who in their right mind, they reasoned, would target Portland, Maine? But as tiny hamlets like Newtown, Connecticut, and Aurora, Colorado, continued to become household names, no one had been able to convince her Portland couldn't eventually join the unwanted list.

And a relationship was out of the question. Who would want to be with someone who couldn't do all the things—go all the places—she no longer could?

"Talking to a therapist helped me get past what happened," Susan said. "Have you thought about seeing someone to talk things out?"

In Jake's line of work, admitting pain was a sign of weakness, and she prided herself on being strong.

"I'm fine."

Susan smiled sadly. "I guessed you'd say that. But if you ever feel otherwise, give me a call, okay? I might not be a professional, but I'm a pretty good listener."

Jake squirmed in her seat, torn between digging deeper into the emotions the conversation was bringing up and changing the subject altogether.

"Tell me about Shy," Susan said. "Mom seems rather fond of her, but she doesn't know much about her."

"Neither do I," Jake was forced to admit, "but she's a hard worker. I'd hate to see her go."

"For professional reasons or personal ones?"

Jake arched an eyebrow. "What has Rita been telling you?"

"She said Shy put the smile back on your face. That's why I came here tonight. I wanted to see you happy and smiling again. I lost a leg two years ago, but you lost something even more important, Jake. You lost touch with who you are. I was hoping to meet the woman who helped you find your way back."

Jake didn't feel like she was back. She felt like she had a hell of a lot of work to do. But Shy made her want to make the effort, something no one else had been able to accomplish. And now Shy might be gone for good. If not today, then perhaps after the test results came in. If the results were positive, Shy's absence would be profound. Both on the boat and at home.

Jake had gotten used to having her around. Instead of preparing to say good-bye in several more months, she might have to do it in only a few more days. Despite her initial anger and lingering disappointment over what had taken place tonight, she didn't want Shy to leave.

❖

The round trip to Boston hadn't been especially strenuous, but Shy felt physically and emotionally exhausted when she parked Jake's truck in the garage close to two a.m. She had come to Portland to make her family proud of her. She had gotten off to a good start, but she was months away from finishing the job. If, that was, she managed to get her job back in the first place.

Her heart felt heavy as she remembered her mother pleading with her not to let everyone down. She knew how much her family needed the money she sent home each week. Her mother needed help with the bills, Danny needed help with tuition for the classes he was taking at a local junior college, and Laura and Federico needed clothes, shoes, and school supplies. Things she was now able to help provide.

But tonight was about more than money. Tonight, for the first time, she had felt how much her mother wanted her to succeed. And at what price. No matter how much she wanted to be with Jake, she couldn't bring herself to let her family down now.

She trudged toward the woodshed to return the keys to Jake's truck. She wouldn't need the pickup on Sunday. After tonight, she wasn't in the mood to go to the festival or anywhere else. She stopped walking when she saw a car parked under the streetlight. Turning toward the house, she noticed the lights in the living room were still on. Jake had company. The kind that might end up staying overnight?

Not wanting to interrupt whatever was going on, Shy pocketed the keys and headed for her apartment. She hadn't made it more than a few steps when she heard Jake's front door open. Jake and a tall redhead came out on the porch.

Standing in the darkness, Shy heard Jake say, "I'll see you Monday afternoon. I hope you still have your sea legs because you're going to need them."

The redhead laughed. "Don't worry. I think I packed them in my suitcase. One of them, anyway. See you Monday."

Jake and the redhead shared a hug, then the redhead got in her car and drove away.

Shy gritted her teeth after the car's tail lights faded into the distance. She hadn't even taken the urine test yet and Jake had already found her replacement. How was she supposed to regain Jake's trust if Jake didn't give her a chance to clear her name?

It seemed the fresh start she thought she had been granted had come to a premature end.

CHAPTER FOURTEEN

Shy mumbled a greeting as she climbed in the truck, then angled her body toward the passenger's side window and closed her eyes. She usually took a quick power nap while Jake made the short drive from her house to the dock in the pre-dawn dark, but today was different. Today they weren't going to work but to Dr. Halloran's office to begin the process of determining if Shy would be cleared to return to the *Mary Margaret* or banned from it for the rest of the season. Perhaps banned for good.

Jake could tell by the rhythm of Shy's breathing that she was pretending to sleep instead of actually dozing. In a way, Jake was relieved. The ruse saved her from having to try to make conversation. She wasn't in the mood for forced cheer. What was she supposed to say on a day when she didn't have the words to express her feelings? Her disappointment that Shy had placed herself in a situation that could end up costing her a job she obviously loved. Her hope that the faith she had placed in Shy when she had selected her over more experienced applicants hadn't been misplaced.

Shy's uncle had sent her to Portland so she could have a chance to escape the negative influences at home that were dragging her down, but those influences had found her here, too, and, once more, she had given in to them rather than resisting their pull. Shy had limitless potential, but she wouldn't be able to fulfill it until she broke the shackles that kept her bound to her old neighborhood. She had to become her own person. As much as she might have liked to, Jake couldn't do it for her. Shy had to find the strength to do it on her own. Lucy's premature departure indicated Shy might have taken steps in the right direction, but her silence today hinted she might not have completed the journey.

Jake had chosen Shy because she had seemed like she had something to prove to everyone who doubted her abilities. Now she had something to prove to Jake as well: that Jake's instincts about her had been right all along.

Jake had managed to secure an appointment for eight thirty, which meant Shy probably wouldn't be taken to the collection area until nine. Jake noticed Nora Dutton, Dr. Halloran's receptionist, eyeing her as she signed in at the front desk. She mentally prepared herself for the inevitable round of questions.

"Morning, Jake. Louie and I missed you at the festival yesterday."

Nora and her husband lived on a farm outside of town and often provided animals when the festival's organizers included a petting zoo to entertain the kids in attendance. The last time Jake went to the festival, one of Nora and Louie's goats chewed a hole in the sleeve of her favorite shirt.

"I couldn't make it. I had some things I needed to do around the house."

"You work too hard," Nora said with a disapproving frown. "Everyone needs a break sometime. You should get out more. It would be good for you."

"So would winning the lottery." Jake completed the sign-in sheet and dropped her pen on the neatly-lined paper. "Maybe I'll see you and Louie next year."

Nora tilted her head in obvious disbelief. "You said the same thing last year."

"Are we done here?" Jake didn't mean to be rude about what was meant to be a gentle rebuke, but she wasn't up for playing Twenty Questions. Not today. And not about a subject this sore.

Nora reached into a desk drawer and pulled out a souped-up tablet computer with a stylus clipped into the built-in holder. "Have your greenhorn verify the information we captured from her the last time she visited the office," she said coolly. "When she's done, she can return the computer to me. Someone will call her when it's time for her to provide a sample."

Nora's voice was as clinical as her surroundings. When she was done speaking, she looked at Jake like she was waiting for her to apologize for being brusque with her, but Jake couldn't bring herself to say the words.

Mainers didn't ask people about their personal lives, but, thanks to the local media attention she and Susan had received in the *Press Herald* after the bombing, she knew her issues were common knowledge. The majority of the people in town wanted to help her get past the trauma she revisited several times a day, while others thought she was beyond help.

Getting past the events of Patriots' Day 2013 was something she needed to do on her own in her own time. She didn't need to talk to a shrink or listen to the admonitions of well-meaning neighbors. What she needed was time to heal. She didn't have a timetable for how long the healing process would take, but two years obviously weren't long enough.

After Shy verified her medical history, she and Jake sat and waited for her name to be called. Jake read a woefully out-of-date magazine while Shy watched one of the morning news shows, though it quickly became clear neither was particularly interested in the entertainment at hand. Jake read the same article three times without retaining a word and Shy didn't react to any of the images on the TV screen. Jake tossed the magazine on the table and tried to find a way to break the uncomfortable silence, but Shy beat her to it.

Looking her squarely in the eye, Shy said, "I don't expect you to take my word for it, but I didn't do anything wrong last weekend and the test is going to prove it. I didn't smoke pot Saturday night, and Lucy wasn't smoking inside the apartment. I asked her not to bring any drugs with her when she came to visit me because I knew you wouldn't approve and I wanted to abide by your rules. She did what she did to spite you and to get me in trouble. Apparently, it worked. If you want to fire me, you'll have to find a legitimate reason because the test will show I'm clean."

When she was done, Shy folded her arms across her chest and waited for Jake to respond.

Jake sat back in her seat, impressed by the force of Shy's conviction. She had never seen or heard Shy speak so passionately about something. Not even her beloved Red Sox. Shy obviously meant every word of her impromptu speech. Jake's gut told her Shy was being honest about what had happened Saturday night, and Jake internally berated herself for letting her emotions get the best of her that night instead of waiting to hear Shy's side of the situation. She had trusted Shy before Saturday night and she still trusted her now.

"I'm clean, Jake," Shy said, still pleading her case.

Jake was tempted to cancel today's appointment, drag Shy out of the sterile office, and catch up on the four hours they had already lost on the water, but she couldn't. They had to go through the process so there could be no doubts. So Jake couldn't be accused of playing favorites. She had to treat Shy like any other greenhorn, even though she was anything but.

So when the nurse called Shy's name, Jake looked at Shy and said, "I hope you're right."

❖

Shy followed the nurse into the holding area and half-listened as he delivered the usual spiel.

"You'll find everything you need in the restroom. First, wash your hands in the sink. Then write your name, date of birth, and today's date on the outside of the plastic container with one of the provided magic markers. Place your sample in the container, secure the lid, and bring the container to me. I'll log in your sample, send it off to the lab for testing, and notify your employer of the results in two to three business days. Do you have any questions?"

"No, I know the drill."

This was, after all, her second test in a little over a month. She was beginning to understand how Charlie must have felt when Jake trotted him in to get tested every time she suspected he was under the influence of something. The difference was, he was using and she wasn't. He had something to hide; she didn't. But she did have something to lose.

"Good luck."

Shy didn't think she'd need luck, but as she closed the restroom door and followed the instructions she had been given, she felt more nervous than she had expected to. She hadn't toked on Saturday. She hadn't even gotten a contact high from the smoke Lucy had blown her way while they stood on the landing. The test she was about to take should be a mere formality, but few things in life came easy. She wanted to keep her job and she didn't want anything to ruin her chances of doing just that. Not Lucy, not the woman Jake had lined up to replace her, and especially not herself.

She had chosen to keep Lucy in her life despite her family's not-so-subtle hints that they wanted her to cut ties and despite her own reservations about her and Lucy's chances of making their relationship a success. Now she might have to pay the price for being stubborn instead of realistic.

After she wrote her name as legibly as she could to reduce the risk of her sample getting mixed up with someone else's, she filled the container with as much urine as it would hold, and screwed the lid on tight.

"Now what?" she asked after she rejoined Jake in the waiting room.

Jake fished her keys out of her pocket and headed to the truck. "Now I drive you home and I go fishing."

Shy wished she could go fishing with her. The lost pay would hurt her wallet, but not as much as not being able to spend the day with Jake would hurt her soul. She hadn't realized how much she had started to enjoy their time together until it was taken away. She'd miss the rhythm, the routine, and the hours of easy camaraderie. Most of all, she would miss Jake.

"Have you already found someone to replace me?" she asked, mentally sticking pins in a red-haired voodoo doll.

"Temporarily."

"Not full-time?" she asked cautiously.

When she'd overheard the conversation between Jake and the redhead, she had assumed they had a more long-term arrangement in mind. She should have done the smart thing and talked to Jake about it instead of jumping to conclusions, but she had been so upset after her argument with Lucy and her conversation with her mother that she hadn't wanted to talk to anyone about anything for fear of being told something she didn't want to hear or allowing her temper to prompt her to say something she couldn't take back. She should have known she could count on Jake to be straight with her, no matter what.

"I won't need a permanent replacement because you're coming back later this week, right?" Jake said.

"I'm planning on it." Shy felt a burden lift. She had spent half the night and most of the morning worrying if she had lost Jake's trust, but Jake's belief in her appeared to be as strong as ever. Maybe her job was safe as well. "So you did believe me when I said I was clean."

"Yes, I did."

"If you believed me, why did you make me go through that whole scene in the doctor's office?" she asked as Jake headed for home.

"It wasn't personal, Shy. It was business. Even though I believe you didn't do anything wrong Saturday night, I need tangible evidence for your employee file. I can't document gut feelings. Otherwise, Charlie's file would be even thicker than it already is. I apologize for flying off the handle this weekend and for putting you through this test today, but I have to follow procedure."

"I get it. I don't like it, but I get it."

Shy looked out the window as Jake drove past buildings and houses that had once seemed so foreign to her but were growing more familiar each day. She waved at Rita heading back into the bank after a smoke break and Micah testing out a beach cruiser in front of his bike shop. Like Lucy, she had once thought she would never feel comfortable anywhere except South Boston, but being here in Portland and the surrounding villages was putting her theory to the test. She felt anxious when she was at home. Like she always needed to be doing something or proving herself to someone. Here, things were different. Here, she could just be.

"What do you want for dinner tonight?"

Jake looked at her out of the corner of her eye. "You're suspended until the test results come back. That part hasn't changed. It's a bit premature to celebrate, isn't it?"

"I've got four days off. I want to make myself useful instead of sitting around twiddling my thumbs. Knowing you, you're going to push yourself extra hard to try and make up for the time you've lost today, which means you'll be exhausted when you get home this afternoon. Let me make you dinner so you'll have one less thing to do. It doesn't have to be anything special. Just whatever you have on hand. What would you like?"

Jake didn't hesitate. "That egg on a horse thing you made with the wine sauce was really good."

Shy couldn't help but laugh at the way Jake mangled the name of the dish she'd made the first time they'd had dinner together. "Steak with an egg on horseback, you mean?"

"Yeah, that." Jake pulled into her driveway, put the truck in Park, and left the engine running. "I've got eggs in the refrigerator, steaks in the freezer, and wine in the pantry. What else do you need?"

"Potatoes and a key to your house if you want dinner to be on the table when you get home." Shy's eyes suddenly went from excited to wary. "If you don't want me in your house while you're not around, I understand. The steaks won't take too long if you'd rather have me wait until you get home before I get started. That way, you can stand watch and make sure I don't—"

Jake didn't let her finish. "There's a bag of potatoes in the pantry and the spare key's in an old jelly jar filled with nuts and bolts in the woodshed."

"Cool. I'll see you tonight. And don't catch them all, okay? Save some for me."

"You got it."

When Shy got out of the truck, she was practically walking on air. Jake felt like a heel for not being more trusting on Saturday. She shouldn't have been so quick to assume the worst when Shy had given her best from the day she set foot on the dock and said, "My name's Ashley Silva. I don't know anything about lobster fishing, but if you give me a chance, I guarantee I will be the hardest-working employee you've ever had."

Bringing Shy on board the *Mary Margaret* had been a gamble, but, for the most part, the gamble had paid off. Could Jake take a similar risk with her heart?

CHAPTER FIFTEEN

J ake could use a cold beer and a hot shower, not necessarily in that order. Both would have to wait, though, because she still had work to do.

"As first days go, this one wasn't so bad, was it?" Susan asked while the day's catch was being weighed.

Jake pondered the question. Susan had fared much better than Jake had expected her to, but she hadn't been able to fill the sizable void left by Shy's absence. Susan had performed her assigned tasks well—her prosthetic leg hadn't held her back too much as she moved around the boat with relative ease despite occasionally rough seas—so job performance wasn't the issue. It was between pots that Jake had missed Shy the most.

Shy didn't talk just to fill the silence as Susan had felt compelled to do today. She got the job done quickly, quietly, and without fanfare. She asked questions from time to time, but only about things that could help her do her job better. In contrast, Susan had kept up a constant patter from their drive to the dock to their return to shore. She had rambled on so much Jake was surprised she still had a voice left. Jake suspected Susan had talked in an attempt to fill the void between them, but her efforts had made the gap seem wider instead of smaller.

Things had been different when they were together. Then, they often went for hours without saying a word because they could practically read each other's minds. As today proved, however, that psychic connection had been severed as neatly as Susan's femoral artery had been the day she almost bled out on the sidewalk in front of a sporting goods store on Boylston Street.

"No," Jake said, "today wasn't so bad."

"But tomorrow will be better. I won't be nearly as nervous now that I have my sea legs back. I'm starting to get the hang of things again, too. There's no way I could do this every day for months on end, but three more days shouldn't be a problem."

Jake didn't think she could take three more days like today. The count had been good, but the fishing itself had left much to be desired.

"I might need you for only two more days if Shy's test results come back early," she said, trying not to sound too eager.

"You're not trying to get rid of me, are you?"

Susan looked hurt so Jake tried to make up for the unintended slight. "I just meant—I mean, I'm sure Mallory would be glad to have you home a day early."

Touching Jake's arm, Susan laughed and said, "We were together for three years, Jake. I can tell when you're lying. Tell Shy her job's safe."

Jake couldn't wait to do just that.

Shy lowered the heat on the wine sauce so it wouldn't reduce too quickly. If Jake stuck to her usual schedule, she would be home in about twenty minutes. Plenty of time for Shy to finish the meal and have it on the table by the time Jake walked through the door.

Shy laughed when she caught herself staring out the window to see if she could spot Jake's truck coming down the street. She felt like a housewife waiting for her partner to come home after a long day's work. She didn't plan on getting used to the feeling, however. Thanks to her family's rules, Jake could never be her partner. Shy's only goal was getting back on the water as soon as she could.

When the sauce had almost reached the proper consistency, Shy began to heat the oil for the steak and potatoes. Jake pulled into the driveway just as Shy was taking the cooked potatoes out to drain. Jake burst through the back door like she was late for something.

"Slow down," Shy said. "Dinner's not done yet."

Jake took off her boots and socks in the mud room and padded into the kitchen barefoot. "Do I have time for a quick shower?"

Shy noticed Jake's face and arms were covered in a thin layer of salt. She wondered if Jake had been forced to take another unplanned scuba dive today to get rid of debris or perform a quick repair on the boat. She wished she had been there to help. Or, more likely, stand on the deck and worry. But at least she would have had Jake's back instead of leaving the job to someone else.

"Go ahead. I haven't started cooking the egg yet."

Jake frowned. "Just one? You aren't staying for dinner?"

Shy had considered and dismissed the idea because she didn't want to intrude. She knew how much Jake valued her privacy. "I wasn't planning on staying, no. All this is for you."

Jake looked touched if a bit disappointed. "What are you going to have for dinner?"

"I plan to nuke the last two slices of leftover pizza from this weekend."

"Stay." Jake said the word with the force of a command but the tenderness of a request. "Since you spent so much time on this meal, you deserve to have half of it. I'll split it with you."

Shy was shaken by the need she heard in Jake's voice. In that moment, she was willing to fulfill any command Jake might give or request she might make.

"Okay," she said, pulling two eggs out of the refrigerator instead of one. "Now go take a shower so I can finish up. You've got ten minutes."

"I'll be back in five."

Jake jogged up the stairs. Shy heard her bare feet thumping across the hardwood floors that led throughout the house.

Unable to control her curiosity, Shy had treated herself to a tour of the house after she let herself in that morning to defrost the steaks.

She had seen the downstairs rooms the night she came to dinner, when it had rained so hard she thought she'd pass Noah's Ark on the way from her apartment, but she hadn't been upstairs until today. The downstairs rooms were generic, as if they were meant for company, but the upstairs rooms were all Jake.

As she tried to figure out a way to stretch a meal meant for one person into a dish that would feed two, she could picture Jake walking down the wainscoted hall lined with pictures of sailboats. After passing the guest room on the left and the "junk" room on the right, Jake would open the door at the end of the hall, which led to the master bedroom.

A plaid comforter covered the bed, the coverlet's colors perfectly complementing the ocean blue walls. The bed itself was handmade, crafted from reclaimed wood that had probably once been someone's barn.

A door on one side of the room led to the master bathroom, where an old-fashioned claw-foot tub pressed against the wall could accommodate Jake's desire for a bath or a shower. Shy felt her pulse speed up as she thought about Jake undressing for either. She felt herself grow wet when she pictured Jake standing under the shower spray, the soapy lather from her honey-infused body wash covering her firm body, slowly sliding down the valley between her breasts toward—

Shy forced her mind to end the fantasy. If she allowed it to play out, she'd have to take a shower of her own. A cold one.

She needed only a few minutes to cook the eggs. She dropped them into the skillet when she heard the water stop running upstairs. By the time Jake walked into the kitchen, the water from her still-wet hair dripping onto her Maine Black Bears T-shirt, the eggs were done and Shy was ready to plate the food.

"Here. Let me help."

Jake grabbed a plate out of the cabinet and held it up as Shy carefully placed the food on it. Jake brought the plate up to her nose and inhaled deeply.

"This smells so good. You have to teach me how to make it so you won't have to do all the work yourself the next time I get a craving."

"I don't mind," Shy said.

Jake was so serious all the time. Shy liked seeing her happy and enjoying herself for once. Knowing she had helped to put the smile on Jake's face made it even better.

While Shy placed the dirty pots and pans in the dishwasher, Jake grabbed enough silverware for two place settings but didn't reach for a second plate.

"You don't mind sharing, do you?" she asked as she sliced the meat.

"No, it's cool."

In fact, Shy thought it was kind of romantic. Except romancing Jake was supposed to be the last thing on her mind.

She grabbed two beers from the refrigerator, popped the tops, and joined Jake at the breakfast bar.

"How were the numbers today?" she asked, trying to take her mind off the fact that she and Jake were sitting side by side.

"Good."

Shy waved her hand to prompt Jake to elaborate. The one-word response answered the surface question, but it didn't fill in the blanks left behind. She couldn't tell if Jake was trying to spare her feelings because her replacement had done such a good job or if she was trying to keep from throwing the new girl under the bus.

Jake speared steak and potatoes with her fork and dragged them through some of the runny egg yolk. "We nearly filled the hold today. We might have if we'd been able to move a little faster. I can't be too hard on Susan, though. This type of work isn't something she's used to. She volunteered to help me out of a bind."

Shy nearly choked on her food. "Susan's the one helping you out? Rita's Susan? *Your* Susan?"

"Mallory's Susan," Jake corrected her.

Suddenly her job wasn't the only thing Shy was afraid of losing.

"She wants to meet you," Jake said.

Shy didn't know if she was ready to come face-to-face with Jake's ex. Seeing her from afar on Saturday night was as close as she wanted to get for the time being. If she met her, she'd be wondering what had brought them together, what had driven them apart, and what she could do to avoid making the same mistake.

"That would be kind of awkward, don't you think?"

"No more so than having my suspended greenhorn offer to make me dinner." Jake smiled at her unexpected good fortune. "I must be doing something right."

"From where I'm sitting, you're doing everything right."

Shy hadn't meant to say the words out loud, but it was too late to take them back. Not that she wanted to. Jake looked like she had never heard them before, and Shy was glad to be the first to tell her, even though she would never be able to tell her the words she wanted her to hear the most.

"Are you and Susan still close?"

Jake thought for a minute. "Not compared to what we once were, no." She almost added, "And not compared to the way you and I are now," but that could have been wishful thinking. "She said to tell you your job's safe, by the way."

"That's good to hear, but I'd rather hear it from you."

Shy tried to smile, but the expression didn't reach her eyes. The slight quaver in her voice revealed how much this week's ordeal was wearing on her. Jake longed to touch her to offer a bit of comfort, but her desire for Shy was so close to the surface she didn't trust herself not to hunger for more.

Even now, her skin prickled from the heat generated by the proximity of their bodies. She held a death grip on her leg with her free hand so her fingers wouldn't be tempted to mold themselves along the curve of Shy's thigh, which rested only a few tantalizing inches away.

"It'll be over soon," she said, but she had no idea when or if her exquisite torture would ever end.

"What would you like for dinner tomorrow?" Shy asked after tonight's meal was done.

You, naked and screaming my name.

"I don't know." Jake cleared her throat to remove the huskiness from her voice. "Surprise me."

"I saw some drumsticks in the freezer. I think you have garlic, lemons, peppers, and red wine vinegar, too. I could make *piri-piri* chicken and grilled corn on the cob. *Piri-piri* sauce is kind of spicy, though."

Shy rested her hand on Jake's arm. Jake felt such a rush of warmth she thought she was about to spontaneously combust.

"That's not a problem, is it?"

Jake shook her head, not trusting herself to speak. She was so far gone, Shy could say she was making mud pies and she wouldn't care. Just as long as Shy didn't let go.

"Cool." Shy's fingers trailed across Jake's forearm as she drew away. "I'll take the chicken out of the freezer and put it in the sink. It should be defrosted by the time you wake up to work on your boat. You can put it in the fridge for me on your way to the shed. I'll work on the marinade tomorrow to make sure I get it just right. Are you sure you like it hot?"

Jake took a long look at the woman who had ratcheted up her temperature even more than the slowly warming weather had been able to the past month.

"I love it."

CHAPTER SIXTEEN

S hy still woke up at the same time each morning, but the days that followed were vastly different than they used to be. Instead of fishing for lobster, she spent her time watching Jake head off to work each morning, letting herself in the woodshed a few hours later, checking out the progress Jake had made on the boat the night before while she fished the spare key out of the jar, then having the run of the house while Jake was away.

Playing chief cook and bottle washer was fun and not nearly as strenuous as hauling traps, but she couldn't wait for Dr. Halloran's office to call so she could finally get back on the boat.

Tuesday passed with no word. So did Wednesday. She was afraid Thursday would, too, but her cell phone rang while she was prepping fish for salt cod stew. When she saw Jake's number on the phone's display, she knew it could mean only one thing. The results were in.

"Doc Halloran's office just called."

The wind was whipping so hard it nearly drowned out Jake's words. She sounded so matter-of-fact Shy couldn't glean any hints from her tone. Did Jake have good news for her or bad?

"And?" Shy prompted her. "What did he say?"

"Well—"

Jake's sigh made Shy's heart lurch in her chest. Had something gone wrong with the test? If it had come back positive,

Shy would demand to take it again. The results might not be enough to get her job back, but at least she'd have peace of mind.

"It appears I'm losing a cook but I'm regaining a greenhorn."

"Sweet." Shy thrust a salt-crusted hand into the air. "I can start fishing again tomorrow?"

"Unless you want to wait until Monday so you can start the week off fresh."

"No," Shy said quickly before Jake could get any ideas about asking Susan to extend her stay. "Tomorrow's fine."

"Just so you know, I'll be paying you for the hours you put in this week. I've already cleared it with Kate."

Shy hadn't set foot on the boat since last week and didn't expect to be paid for the lost hours. Even though she desperately needed the scratch, she wanted to earn it fair and square instead of receiving it as a charitable donation or a supplement to an apology she had already accepted. "Thanks for being so generous, but tomorrow is the only day I'm looking to get paid for. I didn't do any work this week."

"You did plenty. I've got the expanded waistline to prove it."

Shy looked at the salt cod, potatoes, onions, olives, and eggs laid out on the counter. After tonight, Jake's waistline might expand even more. Hers, too. She hadn't eaten this well in years—nor had so much fun doing it.

Preparing the meals, sharing them with Jake, and receiving her praise had made the suspension seem like a good thing. In a way, Shy was sad to see it come to an end. Yes, she would get to spend more time with Jake on the water, but she would lose the time they had started spending together on land. No matter where it occurred, time with Jake was time well spent and she intended to enjoy every second of the time she had left.

"I've got to go," Jake said. "We're coming up on the next string. I've got pots to haul. I'll see you tonight. And don't forget to set your alarm clock. Tomorrow, you get back to the grind."

Shy couldn't wait. "Sure thing, Cap."

After she ended the call, she did a little dance around the kitchen and called her mother to give her the good news. When she finally recovered the hearing her mother's excited scream had temporarily taken away, she looked in the refrigerator to see if Jake had anything she could use to make dessert. Tonight, she felt like celebrating.

She spotted eggs, cream, butter, and milk in the refrigerator, sugar on the counter, vanilla extract in the pantry, and a frozen pie crust in the freezer. Everything she needed to make egg tarts. Everything, that was, except the recipe.

As she took the pie crust out of the freezer to thaw, she debated calling her mother back to ask her for her version of the recipe, but she quickly decided against it. Her mother would most likely ask why she wanted the information. If she let it slip that she wanted to make the dish for Jake, she might let something else slip, too. Something she couldn't afford for anyone in her family to know. That she wanted Jake to be much more than her boss.

Employing a high-tech solution to her problem, she accessed her phone's Internet browser and used the default search engine to find the recipe. According to the directions on the screen, she would have to allow the pie crust to defrost, then roll it flat, brush it with butter and water, roll it up, divide it into several balls, press the balls into a muffin tin, mix the wet ingredients to make a filling, pour the filling into each tart, and put everything in the oven to bake.

The prep time was three times as long as the baking time, but if Shy pulled it off, the results would be so worth it. She smiled as she imagined Jake's rapturous moan after she bit into a tart, its sweet center still warm from the oven. The thought nearly prompted a moan of her own.

She whipped the eggs, cream, and milk with unbridled fervor. Who knew baking could be so inspirational?

❖

Jake pulled her truck into the garage and hopped out. Her stomach started growling even before she made it to the house. She had been looking forward to dinner all day. She had no idea what was on the menu, but she knew whatever Shy planned to dish up would undoubtedly be good. Now that her uncertainty about Shy's future had passed, she would be able to enjoy the evening without feeling like the Sword of Damocles was hanging overhead.

After Susan finally stopped overcompensating, the week had gone much better than Jake had expected. When she dropped Susan off at Rita's this afternoon, saying good-bye was easier than it was the last time they had parted ways. She had thanked Susan for all her hard work this week and told her she had a newfound appreciation for her abilities. Instead of dwelling on all the things Susan could no longer do, she could focus now on all the things she could.

"Then my job here truly is done," Susan had said as her eyes welled with tears.

Happier and more relaxed than she'd been in months, Jake sat on the bench in her entryway and pulled off her work boots. "Hey there," she said after she tossed her socks in the hamper.

The oven beeped, Shy placed a tin of what looked like miniature custards inside to bake, and set the timer for twenty minutes.

"Hey, yourself."

Jake lifted the lid off the soup pot and took a deep whiff of the fragrant stew bubbling inside. The wonderful aroma made her stomach growl even louder. "I think you missed your calling," she said, lowering the lid back into place.

Shy turned to wipe spilled sugar off the counter, but not before Jake saw her start to blush. "If you're trying to sweet talk me into making steak with an egg on horseback for you again, you don't have to try so hard. All you have to do is ask."

"What if I give you this instead?" Jake pulled an envelope out of her back pocket and handed it to Shy.

"What's this?" Shy asked, turning the envelope over in her hands.

"Why don't you open it and find out?"

Shy stuck her finger under the envelope's flap and broke the seal. Her eyes widened when she saw what was inside. "Red Sox-Yankees tickets? Are you serious?"

"The teams are scheduled to play a three-game series in Boston the last weekend in August. You once said you'd always wanted to attend a game at Fenway but never had the chance. One of the guys at the dock bought the tickets but can't use them because his wife booked a Caribbean cruise for the same weekend without telling him first. When he said he wanted to sell them, I grabbed them because I thought you might like to have them."

"Jesus, Jake. Do you have any idea how much these cost?"

"Yeah," Jake said with a laugh. "I paid for them, remember?"

"You know what I mean." Shy tapped the envelope against Jake's arm. Then she looked at the tickets again, even though Jake was pretty sure she had already memorized every inch of them by now. "It's a day game. We could go and be back in plenty of time for you to do some work on your boat. You are coming with me, aren't you?"

Jake's smile faded. She turned and grabbed a bottle of water out of the refrigerator after her mouth suddenly went dry. "Thanks for the offer, Shy, but you know I can't take you up on it."

"I know you don't like crowds, but I still don't know why. Will you ever tell me?"

"One day," Jake said, hoping the day wouldn't come any time soon.

Working with Susan this week had allowed her to put part of her painful past behind her and she didn't want to dredge it up again. She finally felt ready to move on. For her, that meant looking ahead not behind.

Shy's eyes bore into hers, searching for answers she didn't have. This time, Jake was the first to look away.

"I'm going to take a shower."

"Thanks for the tickets."

Shy's voice stopped Jake in her tracks. The kiss Shy pressed to her cheek nearly stopped her heart.

Jake opened her mouth to respond. Not in words but in deed. She ached to kiss Shy. To take her right here in the kitchen of the house Shy had made feel like a home once more. But she couldn't. Not until she was sure her newfound sense of control wouldn't disappear as quickly as it had arrived. Until she could be the woman she once was. The woman she wanted to be again.

"You're welcome."

❖

After Jake went upstairs, Shy stood in the kitchen and listened to the shower run.

When she had kissed Jake on the cheek, she had heard Jake's breath hitch. When she had pulled away, she had watched Jake's eyes darken from a bright blue to a murky navy. She had seen Jake's lips part in invitation then quickly slam shut before she turned and walked away.

Shy now knew for certain what she had almost managed to convince herself couldn't be true: Jake wanted her, too.

Desire told her to take what she had learned, climb the stairs, and tell Jake she felt the same way. Logic kept her rooted in place.

Jake was her boss. Jake was an Anglo. Jake was so many things Shy wasn't supposed to want. So many things she wasn't supposed to be able to have.

Her family had told her to stay away from women like Jake. To be friends with them, but not dream of more. "She isn't one of us," her family would tell her if they could see her now, clutching the sink with both hands and shaking with need.

But her family was two hours away. None of them were here to frown with disapproval and tell her what she was feeling was wrong. None of them were here to stop her from exercising the freedom only distance could provide.

She started for the stairs but stopped herself before she reached them. What if she was wrong? What if Jake didn't want to act on her feelings? If Shy pushed the issue, she could lose the job she had just regained. And she could lose Jake for good.

Then she remembered the feel of Jake's skin beneath her lips. The sound of that interrupted breath. The sight of the hunger in Jake's eyes.

The shrill beeping of the oven timer spurred Shy into action. She placed the tickets on the counter, took the stew off the heat, pulled the tarts out of the oven, and headed upstairs.

❖

The warm water slid over Jake's body like a lover's fingers, stoking her arousal. Every time she closed her eyes, she saw Shy coming toward her, her lips parted for a kiss. In reality, the kiss had been a peck on the cheek. In her mind, it was much, much more.

She lowered the dial on the hot water and her nipples pebbled in protest as the icy needles of the shower spray beat against them. Despite the decreased temperature, Jake still felt like her body was on fire.

She grabbed a fistful of the vinyl shower curtain and braced one hand against the tiled wall. She pinched an almost impossibly hard nipple with the other hand and bit her lip to keep from crying out.

Despite her efforts to remain quiet, she was powerless to stop the whimper that escaped when she imagined it wasn't her fingers but Shy's sliding over the flat plane of her stomach, raking through the trimmed hair at the apex of her thighs, and stroking her clit. That it wasn't her fingers but Shy's making her hips undulate to a rhythm as old as time.

"Let me do that."

Shy's voice cut through Jake's reverie. Jake spun around, unable to separate fantasy from reality. Was Shy really here in the shower with her or was she imagining that, too?

Except for her shoes and socks, which she must have discarded on her way up the stairs, Shy was still fully dressed. Water from the shower spray quickly soaked her T-shirt and doused her jeans.

"You're getting wet," Jake said, watching Shy's white T-shirt turn transparent.

"I've been that way since I kissed you."

"Kiss me again."

Shy stepped toward her. She skimmed her fingertips up Jake's thighs, making the muscles quiver in anticipation. Then she backed Jake up against the wall and curled Jake's leg around her hip.

Jake pulled her closer. Shy's fingers found Jake's clit at the same instant their lips met. Jake moaned at the contact. She didn't know which sensation was more incredible: the feel of Shy's fingers or the taste of her tongue. When Shy slipped first one, then two fingers inside her, she had her answer. She gasped in surprise. In wonder. In ecstasy.

"I'm so close."

She meant the words as a warning so Shy would slow down and they could make the moment last. Instead, Shy pumped her hand faster. She kneaded Jake's breast and dipped her head to take a tumescent nipple in her mouth.

Jake felt herself start to crest. She tried to hold back the inevitable, but when Shy whispered, "Come for me," after painting a line of soft kisses on the side of her neck, Jake exploded against her hand.

Jake's legs started to go, but Shy wrapped an arm around her waist to keep her from falling.

"That was amazing." Shy turned off the water, pulled the shower curtain aside, and reached for two towels so they could dry themselves off. "Are you ready for dinner?"

"No." Jake tossed her towel aside. "I'm ready for more of you."

Shy took Jake's hand and followed her to the bedroom. She felt like she was about to have sex for the first time. In a way, she supposed she was. When she was with someone, she was normally the aggressor. Right now, though, Jake was in charge.

Jake slowly pulled Shy's T-shirt over her head and dropped it on the floor. Shy started to say something about her wet clothes damaging the hardwood floor, but Jake silenced her with a kiss.

"The floors are teak. Teak handles moisture well, remember?"

Shy vaguely recalled Jake saying something along those lines when she'd shown Shy her boat, but all Shy could concentrate on now was the glorious feel of Jake's hands on her skin as they slid up her back and unhooked her bra.

Shy felt goose bumps form on her exposed flesh. Not from the chill brought on by the drying water but from the intensity of Jake's gaze as her eyes took her in. Wanting Jake to see all of her, she unzipped her jeans, hooked her thumbs in them, and pushed them to the floor.

"You are so beautiful, Shy."

Jake's voice was reverent, but her touch was downright sinful.

Kissing her slowly and thoroughly, Jake backed her up to the bed and gently lay her down. Jake's movements were purposeful and unhurried. Shy wasn't used to being able to take her time—or being the center of someone's attention. Jake made her feel special. Desired. Loved.

Jake spread Shy's legs and settled between them. When she parted Shy's lips with her tongue, Shy raised her hips to meet her.

Jake's exquisite mouth drew noises from Shy that sounded more animal than human. The desire building inside Shy was equally feral. When she climbed the stairs, she had thought making love to Jake would sate her need. Instead, she felt like a castaway who had drunk salt water in a futile effort to quench her thirst. The need was stronger now than ever.

She tried to express what she was feeling, but she could manage only one word. One name.

"Jake."

Shy called out for her again and again, each iteration growing louder and louder until, finally, there were no words left.

When it was over, when Shy's body felt like it had come apart at the seams, Jake smiled down at her and said, "Now that I've had dessert, who needs dinner?"

"Me, for one."

Shy finger-combed her tangled hair. She was always good for at least two bowls of fish stew. After the workout she'd just had, though, she might have to go for three.

"Stay right here." Jake kissed the bridge of her nose. "Tonight it's my turn to work for you."

"Don't forget dessert. You might have had yours, but I haven't had mine yet."

"Don't worry," Jake said, bending to give her another kiss. "You'll get your chance."

"I'd better." Shy folded her hands behind her head and enjoyed the view as Jake bent over to pull a T-shirt and a pair of boxers out of a dresser drawer. "Nice outfit, but I think I like your birthday suit better."

Jake found her a similar outfit and tossed it on the bed. "I could say the same about you, but I don't want you catching a cold and calling in sick on your first day back at work."

"You're right. My boss might be pissed if I did that."

"Yeah, I hear she's a real hardass."

"You must have heard wrong. What I heard is she has a cute ass."

Jake grinned, the first smile Shy had ever seen reach her eyes. "We need to talk about where you get your information."

Shy rubbed her bare legs against the sheets. "Do we need to talk about what happens next, too?"

"At some point, but if it's okay with you, I'd rather focus on what's happening now instead of what happens next."

"Fine by me."

The longer they put off having a serious conversation about the future, the longer Shy could delay having to decide if they could have a future in the first place.

Then thoughts of the future quickly came a distant second to concern for the present.

Shy heard a sizzle like the sound fireworks made just before their brilliant colors lit up a night sky. Then a series of explosions ripped through the early evening quiet. Shy's ears rang from the aftereffects of the percussions. When she clapped her hands over her ears to isolate the sound, she realized the noise she heard wasn't coming from inside her head but downstairs.

Jake was screaming.

CHAPTER SEVENTEEN

Shy stumbled down the stairs, feeling her way in the unexpected darkness. By the time she reached the bottom step, the house had grown eerily quiet but the street was a beehive of activity.

She opened the front door and went out on the porch. Jake's neighbors, armed with flashlights and battery-powered lanterns, came out of their houses to see what was going on. Shy peered up the street and quickly spotted the problem. A transformer four or five houses up had blown. The other two transformers sharing the same line had gone up in a rapid-fire chain reaction. The burned wires writhed on the ground, sparks from their live ends setting small fires in the grass.

Most of the houses on Jake's side of the street were completely dark. Shy guessed the power wouldn't be restored for hours.

"Jake, are you seeing this? It's a real mess out there. Unless you have a gas-powered generator, I think we're going to be in the dark for a while."

Jake didn't respond. Shy remembered her bone-chilling scream. She couldn't blame Jake for being scared. If she had been downstairs when the transformers started going off, she might have screamed, too.

She closed and locked the door. She didn't think looting would be a problem, but you never knew. Power outages brought out the worst in some people.

"Jake?"

She hadn't seen Jake milling about in the street, which meant she had to be somewhere in the house. Straining to see in the darkness, Shy slowly made her way to the kitchen.

"Jake, are you in here?"

Shy heard something. Something desperate and small.

"Jake?"

She heard it again. A whimper. The kind a child would make if she were afraid or lost. Shy's apprehension grew as she followed the sound.

"Jake, are you hurt?"

If Jake had stepped on one of the live wires, she could have been electrocuted. Shy had to find her fast in case she needed to call 911.

She moved toward the sink and stubbed her toe on a corner of the breakfast bar.

"Shit." The pain was bad but paled in comparison to her fear. "Jake, answer me."

Still nothing but that damned whimper.

Shy felt around for her cell phone. She had left it on the counter. Wherever the counter was. If she could put her hands on it, she could turn on the flashlight app she had downloaded for free because she thought it was cool but had never had the opportunity to use. It would definitely come in handy now.

Her fingers brushed across something that felt like the appropriate size and shape.

"Got it."

She pressed the phone's power button and scrolled through the display screens until she found the icon she was looking for. She pressed her finger against the screen and the multicolored display morphed into a rectangular beam of bright white light.

Shy held the phone over her head and slowly played the beam across the kitchen. Everything looked normal.

Then she saw Jake lying on the floor, curled into a ball in the corner where the counter formed a ninety-degree angle. Her eyes were squeezed shut and her arms were wrapped around her knees.

"Jake, are you okay?"

Shy ran to her, but Jake didn't open her eyes. Shy placed the phone on the floor, knelt in front of Jake, and reached out to touch her but hesitated, not knowing how Jake would react. But if she didn't do something, Jake might remain stuck in this state for who knew how long.

Shy gently placed her hand on Jake's shoulder. Jake was trembling, her muscles rigid with tension.

"Come back, Jake," Shy said softly. "It's okay. *You're* okay."

Jake's eyes fluttered open as Shy stroked her hair. Shy didn't like what she saw in them: uncertainty and fear. She had seen both before. In her father's cousin, Vasco, who his wife said was never the same after he came home from the Gulf War.

Shy sat on the floor and cradled Jake's head in her lap.

"How long have you had PTSD?"

Jake didn't like using the clinical term for her condition. Posttraumatic stress disorder. Shell shock. Battle fatigue. Three different phrases that meant the same thing. She was broken. Had been for years and might always be.

She closed her eyes again. She didn't want Shy to see her like this. She didn't want to *be* like this.

She had thought finding closure with Susan would put an end to her torment, but as tonight proved, her wounds still hadn't healed.

"My dad's cousin Vasco had flashbacks so bad he'd wake up not knowing if he was in Baghdad or Boston," Shy said when Jake didn't answer. "He'd start reliving battles he was in. He'd think his wife and kids were insurgents and treat them like they were prisoners of war. They started barricading themselves in their rooms at night, but he always found a way in. Finally, they told him they were too afraid to be around him unless he got help. The people at the VA gave him the name of a therapist he could go see to talk things out."

Susan had given her similar advice, but Jake had been too stubborn to take it. "Did it work?"

"I don't know about the talking it out part. I wasn't there for the sessions. But the therapist did recommend something that seemed to help. Vasco started wearing a rubber band around his wrist like smokers do when they're trying to quit. Instead of popping himself with it every time he had a craving, he popped himself every time he felt like he was losing control. He must have gone through a case of rubber bands, but the flashbacks eventually stopped and his family isn't afraid of him anymore."

"I don't think my family's afraid *of* me. More like afraid *for* me."

"What happened?"

Jake knew the time had finally come to stop avoiding the question. She pushed herself into a sitting position.

"I was in Boston on Patriots' Day when the bombs blew up near the finish line."

Beside her, Shy nodded in recognition. In understanding. Shy's quiet acceptance gave Jake the strength she needed to go on.

"Susan was there, too. We were standing right next to each other, but she took the brunt of the blast and I walked away without a scratch."

Jake leaned the back of her head against the cabinet, remembering the fear and confusion. Smelling the acrid odor of smoke and the coppery stench of blood. So much blood. On her hands. On her clothes. On the sidewalk. In the street. And the screams. God, the screams.

She took a breath before she continued.

"Susan lost a leg in the blast. I used my shirt as a tourniquet to keep her from bleeding out before help arrived. One of the race volunteers helped me carry her to the area where a makeshift triage unit had been set up. An ambulance took her from there to the closest hospital that was still accepting patients. She went into emergency surgery right away and was in the hospital for more than a month. I stayed with her the whole time. I didn't care about fishing. I didn't care about anything. My only focus was getting her home. When that day finally came, I thought everything was going to be okay. We had our lives back and we could return to normal."

Jake raked her hands through her hair as she remembered how hopeful she'd been those first days after Susan's release from the hospital. Slowly, that hope had faded.

"I was still committed to the relationship, but cracks started to form, and Susan and I grew apart."

"Were you having problems then, too?"

"My first symptoms didn't appear until two months after Susan and I broke up."

"What are the symptoms?"

"They're usually grouped into three categories: reliving, avoiding, and increased arousal. When you relive, you have flashbacks, hallucinations, and nightmares like your father's cousin experienced. Then you start avoiding the people, places, and situations that remind you of the original trauma. With increased arousal, you have problems relating to other people, you have trouble sleeping, and you're easily spooked. I went to a Sea Dogs game and I started reliving during the seventh inning stretch, right in the middle of a group from one of the local high schools singing 'God Bless America.' I had to leave before the game resumed because I felt like the walls were closing in. The fireworks after the game had me ducking for cover."

"Like tonight?"

"Only worse. I started avoiding soon after."

"That's why you don't go to Sea Dogs games anymore? That's why you won't go back to Boston?"

Jake nodded. "I stay away from crowds and loud noises and I try not to deviate from my usual routine. It helps me cope, but it hasn't helped me forget. Apparently, nothing can."

"Maybe forgetting isn't what you need. Maybe remembering is." Shy took Jake's hand in hers and held it tight. "Let me help you, Jake. Let me help you remember."

Feeling Shy's hand in hers, Jake began to remember something she hoped she would never forget: how it felt to fall in love.

Chapter Eighteen

After the events of the past week, Shy thought she and Jake could use a little fun. The way Jake fingered the rubber band on her wrist as they stood in line for tickets at Palace Playland, however, Shy doubted she was having fun. They had barely gotten started and Jake was already starting to panic.

They were supposed to be taking a walk down memory lane, doing some of the things Jake used to enjoy before dealing with her PTSD forced her to cut herself off from the world. Perhaps going to Palace Playland was asking too much for their first outing. Maybe they should have started with something smaller like a bike ride in the park or a walk along the harbor. Anything but this. The heat, the noise, and the crush of people were too much for Jake to deal with so soon.

"We don't have to do this if you don't want to," Shy said.

"I want to." Jake stopped fiddling with the rubber band and squeezed Shy's hand. "What do you want to ride first?" she asked after they bought a book of tickets. An ambitious fifty instead of a more conservative twenty. Shy would consider the day a success if they used even a fraction of the tickets.

"How about Convoy?" Shy pointed to a ride featuring trucks that carried passengers over a picturesque suspension bridge. "Or maybe Dizzy Dragon?" She indicated four colorful versions of the mythical creatures spinning in a large circle while the passengers inside squealed in delight.

Jake wrinkled her nose. "Convoy and Dizzy Dragon are kiddie rides. I think you and I are above the height limits for both." She looked at Shy, her expression earnest. "I know we're supposed to be testing my limits today, but you don't have to set the bar quite so low."

"Okay then. How about Power Surge?"

"If that's the one Morgan's always raving about, no thanks." Jake shuddered. "You don't have to set the bar quite so high, either."

"Then Pirate may be more your speed."

The ride looked like a pirate ship. As it gently swung back and forth, you were literally lifted out of your seat. When she had ridden Pirate with Morgan, Shy had felt weightless at one point. She couldn't think of a better way for Jake to begin regaining her freedom than by releasing herself from gravity's hold.

As they began to walk the crowded grounds, Shy was tempted to take Jake's hand to offer her tangible support rather than moral, but they hadn't defined their relationship so she wasn't sure how open Jake wanted to be. Was she okay with letting people know they had slept together or did she, like Lucy, prefer to keep it under wraps?

They settled into their seats on Pirate after finally making it through the long line of passengers waiting to board. Jake popped her rubber band against her wrist when the faux ship began to move. She did it with such force the elastic band snapped in two.

"How many did you bring?" Shy asked as Jake quickly replaced the broken rubber band with a fresh one.

Jake patted her bulging front pocket. "Enough." The ride began to pick up speed. "I hope."

Shy didn't want to call attention to what they were attempting to do, but as their fellow riders began to murmur with excitement, Jake looked like she needed some positive reinforcement.

"You're doing great, Jake."

Jake held the safety bar in a white-knuckle grip as a fine sheen of sweat formed on her forehead. "We'll see if you're singing the same tune after I puke my guts out in five minutes."

But Jake didn't puke. Not on Pirate or Drop Zone or Galaxi Coaster. Instead, she sported a smile so wide it threatened to split her face. She went through several rubber bands, but by the time they ran out of tickets, she hadn't depleted her stash.

"Are you ready for Power Surge now?" Shy asked as they shared a large bag of kettle corn from the snack bar.

Jake reached into the oil-stained paper bag and pulled out a handful of the salty popcorn with a hint of sweetness. "Maybe next week."

"Let's go over there." Shy indicated a spot overlooking the beach where they could sit and talk in relative privacy if not quiet. Not with the music from the carousel blaring nearby.

The map of the grounds referred to the area as the town square. The benches didn't look very comfortable, but their nonporous surfaces could withstand the moisture in their jeans, which were still damp from their watery ride in the hollow log boats of Cascade Falls.

"If you want to come back next week, today must have been good for you."

"*You're* good for me. I can't tell you how many times I've wanted to come here with Kate, Tess, and Morgan the past few years, but I was never able to talk myself into it. Now, thanks to you, I might be able to say yes the next time Morgan asks me to come instead of coming up with an excuse to say no. If there is a next time."

"You sound like you think he's given up on you."

Jake folded her arms on the round tabletop. "I wouldn't blame him if he has. I've been a lost cause for a while."

"If that was the case, why did I see so many supportive smiles thrown your way today? You might not have noticed them, but I did." Jake looked at the breaking waves in the distance as if she were replaying the events of the day. "See?" Shy said when she saw recognition light up Jake's face. "I'm not the only one who's pulling for you. I'm not the only one who believes in you."

Jake's eyes grew moist. "Stop before you make me cry."

If Shy had her way, the only tears Jake would ever shed were tears of happiness. Would there be tears when the season ended? She had never been any good at good-byes and she doubted she would handle this one any better than she had any of the others.

"Let's go home," Jake said when the bag of kettle corn was empty.

"Had enough for one day?"

Jake stood and extended her hand. "Today was fun, but I'd rather spend the rest of it making love to you."

Shy took Jake's hand with a hint of sadness. Today felt like a new beginning, but it also felt like the beginning of the end. The season would come to a close in a few months. When it did, she and Jake would be forced to part ways.

Even if it was only temporary—even if Jake invited her to come back next year for another season of fishing—saying good-bye in December would be the hardest good-bye of all.

CHAPTER NINETEEN

Jake was falling behind in the work on her boat. If she kept up her current pace, she wouldn't finish building the sloop by December. Since she already had a January start date to build a boat for someone else, she'd have to stop working on hers so she'd be able to fill her client's order. She didn't want to put her own project on the back burner, but she'd do it in a heartbeat if it meant continuing to sleep through the night and wake up the next morning with Shy in her arms.

The first time she'd woken up after the sun rose instead of several hours before dawn, she'd thought it was a fluke. She'd thought she was just overly-tired from the five-mile hike she and Shy had taken along one of her favorite trails. Then it had happened the next day and the one after. Now it was July and she was still hitting the snooze button each morning instead of shutting off the alarm hours before it even began to sound.

She hadn't worked on her sloop during the week since mid-June. That was before Shy started sleeping over instead of returning to her apartment after they'd eaten dinner and made love—or vice versa. Now Shy spent more time in the house than she did her apartment. Jake supposed they should stop the pretense and make Shy's move official, but their burgeoning relationship was going so well she didn't want to jinx anything by moving too fast.

She and Shy worked during the week and played every weekend. Some destinations were crowded, others practically deserted. Jake never knew where they would end up until Shy stopped the truck and said, "We're here."

The uncertainty kept Jake on her toes. When they left the house, she didn't know if they'd end up surrounded by people or utterly alone. She kept a fresh supply of rubber bands handy just in case, but her anxiety became more manageable each time out.

She wanted to accompany Shy to the Red Sox game in August—Shy said she'd understand if she didn't go, but Jake knew Shy had her heart set on sitting in the stands with Jake by her side.

Jake felt like she was doing better at maintaining control during stressful situations, but she didn't know if she was doing well enough to be able to sit in a crowd of thirty-seven thousand at Fenway. She'd know more after tonight. If she could handle being among nearly twelve thousand fans in McCoy Stadium in Pawtucket, maybe she could handle going back to Boston for the first time since what she swore was the last time.

Traveling to Rhode Island today to see Pete pitch against the Toledo Mud Hens was going to be her next big test. Shy had told her about the trip ahead of time because there would be fireworks after the game to celebrate Independence Day and Shy wanted her to be prepared before the pyrotechnics started going off.

Kate, Tess, and Morgan were making the trip, too. Jake couldn't tell if they were more excited about seeing Pete pitch or having her sit next to them. She'd missed attending games with them, watching them live or die with each pitch Pete threw. Hopefully, today's game would soon become the norm rather than the exception.

As the morning sun streamed through the bedroom window, Jake lay in bed and watched Shy sleep. After she and Susan broke up, she hadn't thought she'd find love again. Not simply because she wasn't looking but because she didn't know if she'd ever be able to open herself up and let someone in. Let someone see the fear and uncertainty she kept hidden during the day but threatened to overwhelm her at night. She hadn't wanted to share her burden with anyone. She had wanted to bear it alone. Then Shy Silva had walked onto the docks, into her heart, and offered to help carry the weight.

"Morning," she said when Shy began to stir.

Shy covered her face with her hands. "I wish you wouldn't watch me sleep."

"Why not?"

"Watching me drool on my pillow can't be very sexy."

"You don't drool." Jake pulled Shy's hands away and gave her a reassuring kiss. "You snore like a freight train, but you don't drool."

Shy pursed her lips. "You've been waiting all night for that one, haven't you?"

"Maybe." Jake brushed a lock of hair away from Shy's face and tucked it behind her ear. "Tell me your fears."

"Why?"

"You're helping me face my fears. I want to help you face yours. What are you afraid of?"

"Disappointing my family."

Jake settled deeper into the pillows. "That's a recurring theme with you. Why are you so afraid of letting your family down? Is your mother one of those tiger moms who won't accept anything less than straight A's?"

"Not quite. When I was in school, my report card had more consonants than vowels."

"What, then?"

"Since my sister and brothers and I were kids, we've been taught to put family first. I've always been able to do that because I didn't have reason not to. Now I do."

"What do you mean? Your family knows you're gay, right?"

"Yes," Shy said quietly, "but they don't know about you."

"And that's a problem?"

Shy laced her fingers around Jake's. "*You're* a problem."

"Why would having me in your life be an issue for them? Kate and your uncle had a great relationship when they fished together. I heard nothing but raves from her about him. If he didn't feel the same way about her, why would he call her to recommend you to me?"

"They had a working relationship, not a sexual one. It was okay for Kate and Uncle Cristiano to fish together. If they had been sleeping together, it would have been a different story. That's why I haven't told my family about you."

"Why? Because I'm not Portuguese?"

"When I was younger, my father made me promise not to bring anyone home who...didn't look like us."

Jake couldn't believe what she was hearing. "Was he stuck in the Middle Ages or something? Did he arrange a marriage for you while he was at it?"

Shy released her hand. "My father wasn't a bad person," she said defensively. "Just stuck in his ways."

"And your mother? How does she feel about it?"

"She's very traditional. To her, the husband is head of the family and whatever he says goes. Even if she disagreed with my father, she would never admit it."

"And now?"

"Now she defers to Uncle Cristiano on most things and he and my dad shared the same views."

Jake's parents were traditional, too—her father had gone to work and her mother had stayed home to take care of the house and kids—but, unlike Shy's parents, they had never tried to place limitations on who Jake or her sister could and couldn't see.

"Is that why you've only dated women of Portuguese descent? Because your family would disown you if you didn't?"

"Pretty much."

A terrible thought occurred to Jake. Try as she might, she couldn't push it away. "Do you ever plan on telling them about me or am I just a casual fling?"

"You know you mean much more to me than that."

Shy reached for her, but Jake backed away.

"Do I? Then tell me what you're going to do when the season ends. Are you going to tell your family about us or are you going to go back to Boston and pretend none of this ever happened, then come back here next year hoping to pick up where you left off?"

"I don't know." Tears sprang to Shy's eyes. "You're asking me questions I don't have the answers to. I want to be with you, Jake, but how can I?"

"Easy. You just do it."

Now it was Shy's turn to pull away.

"It might be easy for you to turn your back on your family, but I can't do it to mine."

Jake stared at her wordlessly, unable to believe someone who had brought her so much joy could say something to cause her so much pain.

"Wait," Shy said. "That didn't come out right."

But Jake didn't wait. She tossed the covers aside, threw on some clothes, and stormed out. Shy let her go.

How could she beg Jake to come back if she didn't know if she was planning to stay?

❖

Jake spent the rest of the afternoon in her woodshed. If Shy asked, she was sure Jake would say she was simply trying to clear her head, but Shy thought it was pretty clear she was trying to avoid her. When she stuck her head inside the shed to ask if the trip to Pawtucket was still on, Jake nearly bit it off.

"Why wouldn't it be? I already told Kate, Tess, and Morgan that we're going. I don't want to let them down. Family's important to me, too, you know."

Jake held her gaze to make sure Shy got her meaning. Then she went back to sawing, shaping, and constructing flat pieces of wood into a structure with more curves than Jennifer Lopez.

Shy remembered the night Jake had taken her hand and trailed it over those curves. And she remembered the countless other nights when her hand had trailed over the curves of the woman who had made them. The curve of Jake's neck as she leaned to kiss her. The curves of Jake's breasts as she arched her back to meet her. The curve of Jake's ass as she molded her body around hers. Now they—and Jake—were out of reach.

The drive to Rhode Island was deathly quiet. Jake said a grand total of six words the whole way. Shy knew because she counted every one of them. She counted broken rubber bands, too. Unfortunately, the total for those was a lot higher than six.

"Is this how it's going to be until December?" Shy asked after they arrived at McCoy Stadium.

"Ayuh, I guess it is."

Make that eleven words.

Jake climbed out of the truck without adding to the tally. She and Shy met Morgan, Tess, and Kate by the Will Call window, where they picked up their tickets. They had seats in the same row, but Morgan wanted to increase his chances of catching a home run ball by sitting on the grass berm overlooking left field rather than in the bleachers.

"I'll go with you." Jake placed a hand on Morgan's shoulder and walked away without looking back.

"Something's off between the two of you," Tess said as she, Kate, and Shy filed into the stands. "Did you have a fight?"

"We're trying to come to terms on something but haven't been able to."

"That's a diplomatic response," Kate said. "You should go into politics."

"Whatever it is," Tess said after they settled into their seats, "I hope you work it out. You've been a godsend for her. For all of us, really. I was beginning to think we'd lost her for good. Lately, though, it's like she never left." She patted Shy's leg. "And I have you to thank."

"Don't thank me yet."

Shy watched Jake and Morgan play catch on the sharply-angled berm, standing with their knees bent and their legs braced so they wouldn't tumble head over heels like the title characters in a nursery rhyme. Shy wanted to be with them. She wanted to be anywhere Jake was. Right now, though, Jake felt a million miles away. And it was all Shy's fault. She should have had the guts to tell Jake about her family's views long before now. Before things had started getting so serious.

She hadn't said anything before they slept together because she didn't think it would ever become an issue. She hadn't said anything afterward because she had known it couldn't help but become one. And now it had.

"Are you coming back next season?" Kate asked.

The answer was once clear. Now, it was a lot murkier.

"If she'll have me."

Pete pitched eight strong innings and left in the top of the ninth with a one-run lead. The closer blew the save, costing Pete the win, but Pawtucket scored twice in the bottom of the ninth to secure the victory.

When the fireworks started after the game, Shy watched Jake instead of the display lighting up the sky. Jake flinched after a few extra loud booms, but she stayed relatively calm.

Shy was so proud, she thought her heart would burst. And it might have if the gaping distance between her and Jake hadn't already broken her heart in two.

CHAPTER TWENTY

Jake wasn't built for temporary attachments. In her line of work, she couldn't afford to be. She needed to establish strong bonds in order to be able to withstand the rigors of her profession. Lobster fishing's physical and mental demands exacted a toll a lover could soothe but only a partner could mend. For a while, she had thought Shy would fill the role. Until Shy let her know she wasn't planning to audition for the part.

As July turned into August, Jake continued to keep Shy at a distance. If their relationship didn't have a future, what was the point in settling for less? But every time she told herself to concentrate on fishing and keep her personal interactions with Shy to a minimum, doubts crept in.

Shy was the first person she had given more than a passing glance since she broke up with Susan two years ago. She didn't know if there was a statute of limitations to being on the rebound. If hers hadn't run out, maybe she was asking too much to try to form a relationship on her first tentative trip back into the dating scene. Perhaps she should kick back and relax and have a few laughs instead of breaking out the U-Haul.

But she wasn't into casual sex and she didn't think she could settle for just being friends with Shy now that they'd been intimate. Not just physically intimate. Emotionally, too. Allowing herself to be weak in front of Shy had allowed their relationship to grow strong.

Now their romantic relationship was over and their professional one was at a crossroads as well.

Jake hadn't made up her mind whether to invite Shy to return next season. The personal strife between them was an issue, but it wasn't her only concern. Like Shy, she had her family to think about, too.

Jeannie, who was due in October, had recently issued Charlie an ultimatum: if he didn't stop using, she would leave him after the baby was born. She had said the same thing before their previous child was born, but this time she didn't sound like she was bluffing. Jake hoped Jeannie would stick to her word. For Charlie's sake as well as hers.

If Charlie got clean and stayed that way, Jake might be tempted to give him his job back. And if he didn't, she'd feel obligated to find a way to help Jeannie get on her feet. Because that's what sisters were for.

Family was as important to Shy as it was to Jake. Shy's obvious love for her family was one of the many qualities Jake found so attractive about her, but it had also torn them apart.

Shy had agreed to her father's unreasonable demand long before she met Jake, so Jake tried not to take the rejection personally. Though she disagreed with it, she understood the intent behind the request.

Shy's father had asked her not to get romantically involved with someone who wasn't Portuguese because he wanted her to respect and remember her heritage, but Shy could do that without being forced to limit who she could and couldn't see. She did it every day. When she worked her ass off on the boat. When she sent money home to her mother to help pay the bills. When she cooked recipes that had been in her family for generations. When she carried herself with dignity, acquitted herself with honor, and treated everyone she met with respect.

Why did she need to adhere to an outdated way of thinking to prove she was proud of her heritage when her actions were proof enough? And, more importantly, why would she let someone else choose who she was permitted to love instead of allowing her heart to make the decision for her?

❖

At the end of another long, nearly wordless day of fishing, Jake stood in her kitchen and stared at the calendar pinned to the wall. The Red Sox-Yankees game was a little over three weeks away. Despite everything, she wished she could make the trip so she could see the longtime rivals go at it in person. So she could smell the freshly-cut grass. So she could hear the crack of the bat when David Ortiz sent a pitch sailing over the outfield wall. So she could feel the excitement of the crowd. So she could see the look on Shy's face the first time she stepped inside Fenway Park. So she could watch the spectacle unfold through her eyes.

She pinched the rubber band around her wrist between her thumb and index finger, lifted it up, and let it snap back into place. The sting of the assault against her skin brought her scattered thoughts into focus. The technique, simple but effective, was slowly giving her back her life. And Shy was responsible. Which made their current estrangement even harder to bear.

Jake took the last bite of her tuna sandwich and washed it down with a swig of iced tea. Then she put her empty plate and glass in the dishwasher and headed to the apartment over the garage.

It was time to bury the hatchet.

She climbed the stairs and knocked on the door. Shy answered a few seconds later. Shy had flour on her cheek from whatever she was making for dinner. Jake longed to reach up and brush it off but forced her hands to remain at her sides.

"Is something wrong?" Shy asked.

Yes. Everything.

"I just wanted to apologize for being such an ass the past few weeks."

Relief washed over Shy's face, erasing the tension that had been evident since the morning their relationship began to unravel.

"No need to apologize. We both said some things we didn't mean to say."

Jake had been told something she wished she hadn't heard, but she hadn't said anything she wished she could take back. Regardless, this was no time to push the issue.

"Do you want to come in for dinner?" Shy asked. "I'm making fried pork with clams."

Jake instantly regretted the hastily thrown together meal she had wolfed down a few minutes earlier. "Thanks, but I just ate."

Shy tried to hide her disappointment but came up woefully short. "Maybe next time."

Jake tried to steer the conversation into safer waters. Relatively speaking. The subject at hand was fraught with its own hidden dangers.

"Did you finally ask someone to go to the Red Sox game with you? The last time we talked, you were still up in the air."

The last time they'd talked, Shy had her heart set on having Jake go with her. Part of Jake held out hope that she still did.

"I'm taking Uncle Cristiano. I started to ask my mom or my sister, but they aren't baseball fans and they'd be bored the whole time. I didn't want to listen to them complain for three hours. My brothers love baseball, but, since I have only one extra ticket, I couldn't ask one without pissing off the other. Lucy and I are still working things out, so I couldn't ask her either. My uncle seemed like the logical choice."

Shy leaned against the doorjamb with a wistful smile on her face.

"My dad and my uncle were starters on their high school baseball team for three years. Their stats were pretty good, but they weren't good enough to impress the scouts who came out to watch them play. Instead of becoming bitter at not being offered professional contracts as some might have, they grew even more passionate about the game. Their love for the sport seeped into me as I grew up watching games on TV with them."

Jake's childhood was similar, but instead of watching the games on TV, she and her father had listened to Joe Castiglione and Jerry Trupiano call them on the radio.

"When I invited him to the game, Uncle Cristiano kept asking me where I got the tickets like he thought I'd bought them from a scalper and we'd be arrested as soon as we tried to use them. He didn't believe they were real until I told him you gave them to me, though I'm surprised he didn't call you to verify."

Jake heard an edge creep into Shy's voice. She wondered how much it was costing Shy to follow a rule in which she obviously didn't believe. Would she forge her own path or would she continue to follow the one that had already been set for her?

But it wasn't Jake's problem anymore. She was Shy's boss, not her lover. And, apparently, that was all she would ever be.

"Have a good time. And if Cristiano asks you about the tickets again, tell him it was a bonus. You've earned it."

And so much more.

❖

Shy's uncle wanted to get to Fenway early so he could watch the teams take batting practice. Shy wished her dad could be here for this, but sharing the moment with her uncle was close enough. His eyes were as wide as a kid's on Christmas morning as he watched the players line up to take their cuts.

"There's Big Papi and Dustin Pedroia." He pointed out two Red Sox players like they were benchwarmers no one would recognize without a program instead of perennial All-Stars. "You see him?" he asked, pointing to a fresh-faced guy with Popeye forearms and legs like tree trunks. "That's—"

"The odds-on favorite to win Rookie of the Year, something no Boston player has done since Pedroia did it in 2007."

Her uncle gave her an appreciative look. "You've been paying attention."

"I had a good teacher."

"Do you think this guy's a keeper? He's hot right now, but he might cool off."

"I doubt it. I think we've got our own Mike Trout," she said, referring to the Los Angeles Angels outfielder, a young player who had been in the big leagues for only a few years but possessed the five tools it took to remain a superstar for years to come.

Shy's uncle sucked his teeth in disapproval. "You would pick someone new school to compare him to. I thought I taught you better than that. Trout's good, but he's no Roberto Clemente. Clemente put the Pirates on his back and led them to the World Series title not once but twice. And he did it eleven years apart. Mike Trout has Josh Hamilton *and* Albert Pujols, and they've never made it to the World Series together, let alone won one."

"That's because Pujols is just starting to get healthy again and Hamilton was done before he left the Rangers."

There were few things Shy liked better than arguing about baseball. Her uncle was her favorite sparring partner. She had forgotten how much she missed their bouts.

"Injuries happen in baseball all the time. When Kirk Gibson played for the Dodgers, he hit a walk-off home run against the A's in the World Series and could barely run around the bases because his legs were shot, but he still got the job done. Pujols should have stayed with the Cardinals. He hasn't done jack since he signed that fat contract with Los Angeles. Players are bigger than they used to be, but they aren't better. In my day…."

Shy prepared herself for a long-winded lecture on baseball history. If her uncle really got going, he'd still be talking when the game started, and the first pitch was still over an hour away. Surprisingly, he wrapped up his discourse by the end of batting practice.

"Come on," he said as the stadium slowly began to fill. "Let's look around before it gets too crowded. I want to see everything

I can because I don't know if I'll ever get back here again. Now that the team's winning again, the sellout streak will resume and tickets will be hard to come by."

Using her camera phone, Shy took pictures of the hand-operated scoreboard, the Green Monster, Pesky's Pole, the oversized logo of a pair of socks carved into the outfield grass, and all the other things she had seen on TV but had never been able to see in person. After she grabbed a shot of the lone red seat, which marked the spot of the longest home run ever hit in the park, she asked a passing stranger to take a picture of her and her uncle standing next to the statue of Ted Williams, the man responsible for the titanic blast.

"Williams was the best hitter in baseball," her uncle said, patting the bronze likeness of the man who was also the last player to finish a season with a batting average above .400, a record no one had seriously threatened since George Brett flirted with it more than thirty years ago.

"What about Babe Ruth?" Shy asked, knowing the question would get under her uncle's skin. No one was allowed to question the Splendid Splinter's greatness around him, no matter to whom Williams was being compared.

"If Ruth hadn't finished his career as a Yankee, he'd be higher on my list. As far as I'm concerned, his stats once he left Boston don't count. But you already knew that." He playfully boxed her ear. "Let's go to the concession stand. For daring to invoke the Curse of the Bambino, you owe me a Fenway Frank."

"Don't be such a cheap date, Uncle Cristiano. Let me get you a Monster Dog instead."

"Thanks for being so generous. And thank Jake for the tickets. I owe her one. Make that two." He draped his arm across Shy's shoulders and pressed a kiss to her temple, something he hadn't done in years. Usually, he was too busy trying to shake some sense into her to show her affection. "Are you enjoying your job?" he asked after she paid for their purchases and they finally took their seats.

"Yes, sir."

His thick eyebrows inched toward his balding pate. His semicircular fringe of dark hair, paired with his secular attire, made him look like a defrocked monk. "Sir?" he said between bites of his oversized hot dog. "That's new. Did Jake convince you to start saying 'sir' and 'ma'am'?"

"In a way."

The professional manner in which Jake went about her business made Shy want to follow her example.

"I said you could learn a lot from her. Was I right or was I right?"

"You were right." *In more ways than you know.*

"Let me see your hands."

Shy put down her pot roast sandwich and extended her hands, palms up. Her uncle examined them like a jeweler inspecting a diamond for flaws.

"A few calluses. No cracked skin. Not yet, anyway. Fall's coming soon. Make sure you keep your hands moisturized so they don't split on you. Once they do, it'll take forever for them to heal."

He showed her the deeply etched lines on his palms, battle scars from the rugged winters he had spent hauling pots.

"I'm proud of you, Ashley. You're a sea dog now."

His eyes were misty as he sat back in his seat, but he pointed at his hot dog as if the spicy mustard he had slathered all over it was to blame instead of the emotion of the moment. He cleared his throat and quickly dragged the back of his hand across his eyes. She pretended not to notice so he wouldn't be embarrassed.

"Keep up the hard work and Jake will almost certainly invite you back next season. She might even make you a permanent member of her crew. Would you like that?"

"For a while, I did. Now I don't know if I want to go back."

"You're making good money, you're staying out of trouble, and you're learning a trade. Why wouldn't you want to go back? I know the work is hard, but—"

"It's not the work."

"Are you scared of competing with Jake's brother-in-law if he tries to get his job back?"

Charlie had lost his job because he couldn't stop getting high. He had entered rehab the week before and was supposed to be in the program for nearly a month. He would want his job back when he got out and, because he was family, Jake might feel obligated to give it to him. Shy didn't think Jake would ever return to a three-person crew since the two of them had proved the work could be done just as well with a team of two. If Jake chose to work with Charlie instead of her, Shy would have to try to latch on with someone else, which she didn't know if she was willing to do. She didn't want to work for another captain. She wanted to work with Jake.

"Charlie is physically stronger than I am, but I can work rings around him. In a fair competition, I know I can beat him."

But when family was involved, nothing was fair.

"If it's not the job, then what is it?"

Shy could argue about baseball with her uncle all day, but she didn't want to get into a confrontation with him about Jake for a single second.

"It's…complicated."

"That usually means a woman is involved. Is there?"

Shy didn't want to tell her uncle about her feelings for Jake because she didn't want to hear him denigrate something that had meant so much to her. Her relationship with Jake was dead and buried. She didn't need him to throw any more dirt on its grave.

"I was seeing someone, but it didn't work out."

"Was she Portuguese?"

Shy shoved a handful of French fries in her mouth, hoping they would muffle her response. "No."

"That's why it didn't work out."

"Haven't you ever dated anyone who wasn't Portuguese?"

"Once upon a time."

"Really?" Shy had never heard this part of his history and wanted to know more. "When?"

"I played the field a little bit when I was younger, thinner, and had more hair."

"Why did you stop?"

"Because I knew it wouldn't last. I had some good times with the women I was seeing, but I knew I wouldn't marry any of them."

"Why not?"

"Our differences were too much to deal with on a daily basis. I had to explain too much. Things someone who shared my culture would already be familiar with. What I'm trying to say is you can date anyone you like, Ashley, but you want to marry someone you don't have to teach. Someone who understands you."

Shy remembered Lucy telling her nearly the exact same thing the night Lucy had tried to explain why she had tried to insert a wedge between Shy and Jake.

"She could never understand you like I do," Lucy had said.

But the person who was supposed to understand Shy the least seemed to be the one who understood her the most. And teaching Jake about her culture had been a pleasure, not a chore. A pleasure she wished she could continue to experience.

"So if it's not the work and it isn't a woman, what's the real reason you don't want to go back to Portland?"

Shy was out of excuses and frustrated by her inability to rely on the truth.

"You and Mom sent me to Portland to toughen me up and help me learn to be responsible. Congratulations. It worked. I can continue my self-improvement project at home. Why do I need to go back to Maine?"

"Watch the attitude, okay? You need to go back to Portland because you went up there to do a job and the job's not done. You're just getting started. You can't quit now. If you do, you're going to fall right back into the patterns that got you into trouble in the first place."

"I'm not seeing Lucy anymore, if that's what you're worried about. The way she and I left things was pretty definitive. I doubt we'll ever be as close as we once were."

"Thank God for small favors." Her uncle raised his hands to the sky in mock praise. "But just because you've stopped sleeping with Lucy doesn't mean you're going to stop seeing her. The two of you live in the same neighborhood. You have the same set of friends. You're bound to run into each other from time to time. When you do, she's going to be the same bad influence on you she always was."

"If I let her. You act like I don't have a choice, Uncle Cristiano. I have my own mind, you know."

"And it sounds like you've already made it up. Be smart, Ashley. Don't throw away a good thing just to prove a point."

"Too late," she said. "I think I already have."

CHAPTER TWENTY-ONE

Anthony Kyle Stephenson was born the day his father completed rehab. Even though Anthony made his way into the world two weeks early, he still managed to tip the scales at over nine pounds. If he had stayed in the womb for the full thirty-eight weeks, Jake mused as she stared at her newborn nephew through the nursery window, Jeannie might have given birth to an offensive lineman instead of an infant. Based on Anthony's chubby cheeks and meaty limbs, she still might have.

"Eat your Wheaties, kid. The Patriots might come calling in a few years." Right about the time Tom Brady's son stepped in to play quarterback.

Jake tapped the window with her fingernail to get Anthony's attention. His dark gray eyes opened wide, then quickly squeezed shut as he opened his mouth in a gaping yawn.

"Hey, little man," she whispered to his sleeping form. "Being born is hard work, isn't it?"

"It sure is, Cousin Jake," Charlie said in a childlike voice after he left Jeannie's crowded hospital room to come and stand next to her. "Now will you give my daddy a job so my mommy will be able to stay home with me like she did for my brother and sisters?"

Jake tried to be diplomatic. "I'm not going to make any decisions about next season until next season. I still have this season to finish."

"Next season doesn't start until May. I need to get some money coming in before then."

Jake took a deep breath to quell her growing anxiety. She had hated hospitals even before she'd practically moved into one during Susan's recovery. Despite the happy occasion of her nephew's birth, she didn't want to be here now. The added pressure Charlie was exerting wasn't helping. She resisted the temptation to reach for the rubber band around her wrist, however. She needed to learn to handle pressure without it.

"I understand where you're coming from," she said evenly, "but my crew for this season is already set. I'm not looking to make any changes."

Charlie looked at her, his eyes clearer than she'd seen them in years. It was too soon to tell if rehab had worked, but the early signs looked good.

"I'm not asking you to fire Shy and hire me. All I'm asking is if the time comes, you give me a chance to win my job back fair and square."

"*If*? Are you considering other options?"

If he was, it could make her upcoming decision a hell of a lot easier.

"Like I said, I need to make money now. I've been away from home for a while. Right now, all I want to do is go home, get settled, and hug my kids. Tomorrow or the next day, I'll try to find a spot with someone who fishes year-round so I won't have to worry about making ends meet for five months while you're shut down. But if I can't, I hope you can find it in your heart to give me a chance to fight for a place on your boat next season."

Jake wanted to believe Charlie meant what he was saying, but she'd been down this road with him before and was leery about traveling it again.

"The last time we saw each other, you said you didn't want to work for me."

He grimaced at the reminder, then dragged his fingers through the heavy beard he had grown while he was away. At the moment, he looked more like a lumberjack than a fisherman.

"I said a lot of mean, hurtful things while I was under the influence. To you and a lot of other people. They're things I can't take back."

Jake noticed he didn't say he hadn't meant what he had said. Just that he regretted saying them. Kind of like a convict who didn't regret his crime. Only getting caught.

"One of the steps in my rehabilitation process is to make amends to all the people I've hurt over the years. I want to start with you."

She would have preferred he start with her parents by paying back all the money he had wheedled out of them, but he needed a job for that. Something that, thanks to his track record, few might be willing to offer him.

"I will take every wrong I have ever done to you and make them right. Just give me a chance."

Jake remained skeptical. "No promises? No guarantees? Just a chance?"

"That's all I ask."

Charlie held out his hand. Jake considered it for a long moment before she gripped it in hers.

"It's a deal."

❖

"Relax. You're doing fine."

Shy was so surprised to hear Jake speak this early in the day, she nearly steered the boat into the rocks. Jake didn't normally do much more than grunt until she'd had her third cup of coffee, and she was only halfway through her second.

Shy corrected her course and continued out to sea. For the past month or so, Jake had been giving her more and more responsibility. Not all at once so she'd feel overwhelmed, but a little at a time so she could gradually adjust to the changes. Today, she had been tasked with the challenging chore of taking the boat out in the early morning dark instead of driving it home in the bright afternoon sunshine.

Shy wiped condensation off the window and strained to see where she was going. The fog lights on top of the boat helped penetrate the darkness and the radar screen in the helm helped her get her bearings, but she couldn't wait until the sun rose so she could see more than a few feet in front of her. Maybe the rising sun would bring the temperature up with it. In November, the thermometers in Maine didn't usually get any higher than the low fifties. Today, they were supposed to top out at forty-five. When the wind whipped up, though, it would feel a lot colder than that. If she had known the summer would pass so quickly, she would have tried to enjoy it more.

"I need to make some decisions about next season and it's no secret Charlie wants his job back so he can have a chance to redeem himself."

Shy tightened her grip on the throttle. "Are you going to give it to him?"

"I'm not going to *give* anyone anything. Anyone who sets foot on my boat has to earn his place. Or hers."

They hadn't discussed whether Shy planned to come back next season. With only a few weeks left in this one, Shy assumed the discussion was about to happen whether she wanted it to or not.

Jake topped off her coffee with a fresh infusion from the large to-go box she picked up each morning from a bakery that had been servicing the fishing fleet for nearly fifty years.

"I know things have been strained between us the past few months, but I hope I see you up here next season. You're a natural at this job."

"Thanks."

The compliment helped Shy relax into her new role. She didn't feel quite so much like a deer in headlights as they moved further and further away from the safety of the harbor.

"That chair fits you. Have you thought about getting your captain's license?"

Shy hadn't considered running her own boat one day. Now that Jake had put the idea in her head, she couldn't think of anything else. "Do you think I'm ready?"

"Not yet, but soon. You're smart, you're motivated, and you have a feel for fishing. You've definitely got what it takes to be a good captain."

"Cool."

"We had a few peaks and valleys this season, but the overall numbers have been good. So good I might be able to talk Kate into investing in a second boat or bringing a second captain on board so the company can run the *Mary Margaret* year-round."

"You wouldn't fish the winter season?"

"I've got boats to build. But I would make sure this boat was in good hands before I left her for five months. I could use your help. I'd love to keep you on in either a full- or part-time capacity, but I'd understand if you decided not to stay."

It was hard for Shy to work in such close quarters with Jake yet have her feel so far away. How could she possibly deal with that for the months, maybe years it would take for her to learn enough to branch out on her own? She didn't think she had it in her.

"If fishing is what you want to do with your life, go for it," Jake said. "Don't let what happened between us stop you from pursuing your dreams."

"I won't."

But there was one dream she couldn't allow herself to pursue: making a life with Jake.

They were quiet for the rest of the trip out to the fishing grounds, the only sounds the chugging of the boat's engine and the crashing of the waves across the bow.

As Jake hauled in the first pot of the day, she realized Shy had never answered her question. She still didn't know if Shy planned to come back next spring of if she was interested in sticking around to fish next winter, providing Kate okayed her plan.

Jake found Shy's lack of a response telling. She had been dreading saying good-bye in a few weeks, but perhaps it was for the best. Because it was obvious Shy couldn't make a commitment. Not to the boat, not to a career, and especially not to her.

CHAPTER TWENTY-TWO

Jake flipped the switch on the hydraulic lift. "Last pot of the season," she said as Shy waited for the trap to break the water's surface. "Let's make it a good one."

Shy grabbed the trap, opened the door, and began to sort the lobsters inside.

"One egg-bearing female and three keepers."

Shy cut a notch into the female's tail, tossed her over the side, and dropped the keepers in the hold with the rest of the day's catch after taping their claws shut. Then she secured the trap on the deck instead of rebaiting and resetting it as she'd done five days a week for the past seven months.

After they offloaded today's catch, they would need to take all the traps to the storage unit. It seemed like just yesterday they had taken the traps out of storage. Now it was already time to put them back in again.

Each season seemed to pass faster and faster. This one seemed to pass the fastest of all. Usually, Jake couldn't wait for the season to end so she could wake up without the uncertainty of what each day would bring. This year, she wished she could turn back the clock and start the season over. So she could see Shy's defensive demeanor soften. So she could watch Shy become more comfortable in town, at work, and with herself. So Jake could fall in love with her all over again.

Instead of taking her seat in the captain's chair like she did most afternoons, Shy stood on the deck like she was waiting for something.

Jake cut the power to the lift. "What's up?"

"On TV, the captains always do something special to celebrate the end of a season. Aren't we going to shoot off fireworks or bite the head off something raw to commemorate the occasion?"

Jake laughed at the usual disconnect between reality TV and real life.

"I plan on going home and having a beer, but you can celebrate any way you like."

"Oh." Shy reluctantly joined her in the helm. "I have too much stuff to do anyway. I don't have time to party. I need to close my accounts at the bank, then go home and pack."

Jake found it interesting Shy referred to Portland as home when she didn't seem to want to make a life here.

"What time does your train leave?"

"Tomorrow afternoon at twelve forty-five."

"Do you need a ride to the station?" Jake didn't turn to look at her. If she did, she thought she might cry. Shy's departure, once so far away, was now less than a day from coming to pass.

"I've got one. I've already arranged for a cab."

"Cancel it. I'll drive you."

Shy carefully maneuvered the boat away from the fishing grounds and directed it toward the distant shore. "I don't want to bother you."

"It's no bother."

"But I know you're busy working on your boat."

"It's okay. I'm almost done."

All she had left were a few finishing touches. The additions were cosmetic, though. The boat itself was ready for the water as is.

"Do you have a name for it yet?"

Jake hesitated. "I'm kicking a few ideas around, but I haven't settled on one yet."

"You will."

Shy gave her a look filled with such devotion and trust, Jake wondered yet again why she was so willing to walk away from what they could have—what they could be—together.

Jake kept telling herself to give up on Shy and let her go, but her heart refused to listen. Shy had done so much for her—meant so much to her. She couldn't walk away without putting up a fight.

And she had one more night to convince Shy their relationship was worth fighting for.

"Come to my place for dinner tonight," Jake said. "You don't want to cook on your last night, do you?"

"Not really."

"Then I'll whip something up for you. It might not be as good as anything you might make, but at least you won't have to clean up afterward."

"True. What time would you like me to come over?"

"Let's shoot for eight thirty. That should give us enough time to get offloaded, swing by the bank, store the pots, then shower and change."

"I'll be there."

Jake's invitation to dinner came as a surprise to Shy. It was the first indication Jake planned to treat today as something different. Something special. Because today wasn't like any other day. It was her last day. Her last day of fishing. Her last day in Portland. Her last day with Jake.

She rang the doorbell that night not knowing what to expect. What she wanted was one last night in Jake's arms, but she doubted she would receive it. At this point, reliving the past would be even more painful than remembering it.

Jake seemed out of breath when she opened the door. Like she'd been caught in the middle of trying to do a million things at once.

"Do you need me to do something?" Shy asked.

Assaulted by memories of their time together—some good, some bad, and all of them unforgettable—she followed Jake inside the house.

"No, I'm good. Everything's already set up in the dining room."

Shy wished they were eating in the kitchen for old times' sake. She remembered sitting with Jake at the breakfast bar the first night of her suspension. Sharing a plate with her and swapping stories about each other's lives. Feeling their mutual attraction grow.

Shy had felt so close to Jake that night. The bond had grown even deeper the first night they had made love. When the neighborhood had lost power and Shy had found Jake curled into a ball on the floor. Jake had opened up to her then in a way Shy suspected she had with only a relative few. Shy considered herself privileged to be one of them.

"Can we eat in the—"

"I forgot to grab the wine." Clearly distracted despite her assertions she had everything under control, Jake headed to the kitchen. "Go on in the dining room. I'll meet you in there."

"Sure thing."

Though the rest of the house was brilliantly lit, the dining room was pitch-black. Shy felt around for the light switch. When she found the button and flipped it on, the room flooded with light.

"Surprise!"

Shy's heart filled her throat as she took in the faces of all the friends she had made since she had arrived in town. Kate. Tess. Morgan. Zach. Rita. The tellers from the bank. Micah from the bike shop. The nurses from Dr. Halloran's office. Eleanor Parker from the Sew and Sew and her daughter, India, the future greenhorn. Even Charlie and Jeannie and Susan and the woman Shy assumed was Susan's partner now that Jake was no longer in her life. They were all there. Them and so many more. They had all come to see her. They had all come to say good-bye.

When she looked up at the We'll Miss You banner taped to the wall, her eyes filled with tears. She was a tough girl from one of the toughest neighborhoods in South Boston. She wasn't supposed to cry. But the person she had been in May wasn't who she was now. So when everyone began to come up to her and tell her how glad they were to have met her, when she realized how much time and effort Jake had put into making the whole thing possible, she felt her composure begin to slip. Then Jake made her lose it completely.

After completing her faux errand, Jake tapped a fork against her wine glass to get everyone's attention.

"First of all, I would like to thank everyone for coming. You could have been anywhere tonight, and I'm glad you decided to spend the evening in my home. I wish it were a happier occasion, but we can't have everything, can we?"

Despite the crush of people, Jake seemed relaxed and composed. Like the events of the past that had held her back for so long were now only distant memories. Shy stood in awe of her transformation.

"Secondly, I'd like to thank Kate, Tess, and my mom for cooking all the wonderful food I'm currently keeping you from eating. I know you've been waiting a while to dig in and you're all probably starving by now, but you'll have to wait a little longer. I've been economical with my words over the years because I've been saving them up for tonight. So get comfortable. I might be up here for a while."

Shy looked around. The guests didn't look put out by being made to wait. They looked proud that Jake had finally emerged from the cocoon she'd been trapped in for the past two years. Shy was proud of her, too. Proud and desperately in love.

She had known she was in love with Jake for months now, but the depth of her feelings continued to surprise her. She could feel her love for Jake welling inside her, threatening to spill out. Was it obvious? Could anyone else see? How could they not? Every look, every glance, every touch. Everything she had done while she was here was informed by her love for Jake. Now she would be taking that love with her. Boxing it up like a souvenir.

She didn't want to remember how it felt to love Jake and be loved by her. She wanted to keep feeling it every day for the rest of her life. But her life was in Boston. Where it had always been. Where it would always be.

"Most of all," Jake said, "I would like to thank Shy for all the hard work she put in this season. She came in with no experience, but she swore if I gave her a chance, she would be the hardest-working employee I've ever had. Not only did she fulfill her promise, she exceeded it."

Shy didn't turn to gauge Charlie's reaction to Jake's words because she couldn't pull her gaze away from Jake's eyes. She could practically feel their caress.

"Shy has been a valued employee and an invaluable friend. To me and everyone else here tonight. I, for one, am honored to have known her." Jake raised her glass. "To Shy."

"To Shy," everyone echoed.

Shy couldn't take any more. Despite the bitter cold, she ran outside to get some air. To get away.

"Are you okay?" Jake asked when she came to check on her.

"I'm fine. It's just—" Shy dried her eyes and took a deep, shuddering breath. "I didn't realize how many people I'd come across since I've been here or how many of them cared about me. It got to be a little too much."

"I know how you feel."

"I'm sure you do." Shy thought about Jake's struggles with PTSD and the efforts she had made to free herself from its effects. She had no doubt Jake would win the battle. She only wished she could stick around to watch her do it. "Did you mean everything you said tonight?"

"Every word."

"Then do me a favor."

"Anything."

"Don't take me to the station tomorrow. I can only say good-bye to you once. Let me do it now. Tonight."

Jake's shoulders slumped as if she had been expecting—hoping—Shy would say something else. "If that's what you want."

"It's not what I want, but it is what I need. Thank you for everything you've done for me. Thank you for taking a chance on me. Thank you for loving me. I will never forget this summer. I will never forget this town. I will never forget the people in it. And I will never, ever forget you."

The sadness in Jake's smile was heartbreaking. "You sound like you're leaving forever."

"Because I am." Shy's tears begin to fall anew.

"It can't be forever." Jake cupped Shy's face in her hands and used her thumbs to wipe away her tears. "I still owe you a ride, remember? Come with me." Jake took Shy's hand in hers, her touch achingly familiar. "I want to show you something."

Jake led her to the woodshed. She opened the door but didn't turn on the lights.

"Close your eyes."

After Shy did as Jake asked, Jake carefully guided her inside the shed and closed the door behind them.

"On three," Jake said. "One. Two. Three."

Shy heard the fluorescent lights power on. She opened her eyes, blinking against the sudden glare. Jake's boat sat before her. Not half-finished or nearly done but complete. The sails, mast, and boom were missing because the ceiling was too low to accommodate them, but Shy saw the thick canvas material neatly folded in a corner, waiting to be attached to the wooden support beams resting nearby.

"Jake, she's beautiful."

Jake slowly ran her hand over the hull. "Why do you think sailors call boats she?"

"When are you going to take her out?"

"That depends."

"On?"

"You. I said you would be the first passenger. Whenever you're ready, we'll take her out. Together."

Together. Shy didn't think she had ever heard a word that sounded so good.

"Have you named her yet?"

Jake nodded. "I followed Kate's example. She named the *Mary Margaret* for a woman who meant a great deal to her and I named my boat for a woman who means everything to me."

Following Jake's eyes, Shy walked around to the other side of the sloop, where the words "Shy Girl" had been painted in bright red letters.

"You named her after me? Thank you, Jake."

Jake hesitantly leaned forward and kissed her lips. "Don't thank me, Shy. Just come back."

Chapter Twenty-three

I knew you'd come back."

Lucy greeted Shy with a hug as the arriving and departing passengers in Boston's North Station milled around them. Shy didn't know what to make of the rare public display of affection. Either Lucy had missed her or she'd had a change of heart or both.

"Is this everything or do you have another bag?" Lucy asked after she let her go.

Shy tossed her duffel over her shoulder. "This is it."

"You've been gone forever. I thought you'd have more stuff."

The most valuable things Shy had brought back with her weren't possessions but memories. Scores of memories so vivid they almost didn't seem real. She couldn't carry those in a duffel. She carried them where there was infinitely more room: in her head and in her heart.

"Got a hot date?" she asked on the subway after Lucy checked her watch for the third time in the past five minutes.

"Maybe." Lucy flashed a crooked smile as she held on to the hang strap above her head. "I'm supposed to keep you away from home for another twenty minutes to give your mother and your uncle enough time to get set up. They're throwing you a surprise welcome home party I wasn't supposed to tell you about. Oops."

Lucy covered her mouth with her hand but didn't look the least bit apologetic. Her mischievous smile reminded Shy of Morgan whenever he said something that made his moms laugh or shake their heads in amused disapproval. Shy wondered how much of a handful he would become in a few years. As long as he had Kate and Tess in his life and Jake nearby to pick up the slack, he'd be sure to follow the right path.

Shy was going to miss watching Morgan grow up. But if Pete continued to progress, she'd be able to follow his career. In Pawtucket for now and perhaps Boston in the not so distant future. She couldn't wait to buy a Red Sox jersey with his name on the back.

"Since you already know about the party, why don't we go to my place and get blunted to help you prepare for it?" Lucy asked. "We could have a little party of our own."

In the past, Shy would have gladly taken a few tokes to dull the pain. But Jake had shown her by example there was no pain that couldn't be overcome. Jake had also shown her how empty sex without love—real love—could be. Now that she knew the difference, she refused to go back.

"No, thanks, Luce. I just want to go home."

"Your loss."

"No," Shy almost said. "My gain."

"Are you going to keep staying with your mom or are you going to find a place of your own?" Lucy asked after the subway car slowed to a stop and the doors slid open.

"I haven't thought about it yet." Shy had gotten used to living by herself. She would need time to adjust to sharing a room and a bed again, but having her sister close by might stem the loneliness she had started to feel as soon as the passenger train left Portland behind.

"If you want to move out, you could always move in with me," Lucy said.

"What happened to Carolina? You've been rooming together for years."

"She's moving out to shack up with her boyfriend. She says he popped the question, but I haven't seen a ring yet. I'm in the market for a roommate and you need a place to stretch your newfound wings. What could be more perfect?"

Shy didn't answer right away. She'd just gotten home and she was already beginning to feel trapped. She needed space. Room to breathe. But agreeing to move in with Lucy might be like consenting to take their relationship to a level she no longer wanted to attain. If she set some ground rules, though, perhaps it could work.

"Let me think about it, okay?"

"Sure," Lucy said brightly. "Take all the time you need."

Shy walked up the street of her block, feeling at home and out of place at the same time. When she climbed the front steps of her house and opened the door, she smelled the welcoming aroma of a big Sunday dinner, the kind her mother made only on special occasions.

When everyone yelled, "Welcome back," and rushed forward to greet her, she felt like a conquering hero.

"Do you have anything to say?" her mother asked after Shy hugged everyone in sight.

Shy ruffled her little brother's hair the way he said he hated but she knew he secretly loved.

"Ayuh, I do." She ruffled Federico's hair again. "It's good to be home."

After the party died down a little, Shy went to the room she shared with her sister, Laura, and began to unpack her things. Laura had taken over the whole room while Shy was gone so Shy had to search hard to find room for herself. When she was done, she sat on the edge of the bed and pulled out her phone. She thumbed through the dozens of pictures she had taken over the past seven months. Separately, each photo captured an individual memory. Together, they served as a chronicle of the time she had spent away.

"I want to see," her mother said from the open doorway.

Shy patted the spot next to her. After her mother joined her on the bed, Shy held the phone so both of them could see the screen. As each picture popped up, Shy related where they had been taken and who or what was in them. When she got to the selfie she had taken of her and Jake standing in front of a boat with her name painted on the hull, she ran out of words.

"And that's Jake," she said for lack of anything better to say.

"You love her very much, don't you?"

Shy started to protest but nodded and said nothing.

"Cristiano told me you were involved with someone when you were up in Portland, but he said the two of you had broken up. Was Jake the one you were involved with?"

"Yes." Shy's voice cracked as if she was using it—finding it—for the first time.

"Even before Cristiano said something, I knew."

"How?"

"Because I know you. The night you came to see me, I could hear it in your voice when you talked about her. Now I can see it in your eyes. Which makes me wonder what you're doing here without her."

"Mama, you know how it is. How Daddy felt. How Uncle Cristiano still feels. Why would I put Jake through that?"

"It seems to me you already have. You broke up with her because of what your father asked you to do. What your uncle wants you to do. The only question you should be asking yourself is what you want to do. Do you love Jake?"

"Yes." Shy felt the bonds holding her back begin to loosen.

"Is she worth fighting for?"

"Yes." Shy felt a weight slide off her shoulders.

"So I ask you again, Ashley." Her mother rubbed her back in slow, soothing circles like she used to do when Shy was a kid and she woke up crying from a nightmare. "What are you doing here when your heart is there?"

❖

Jake unrolled the blueprints she had designed for the boat she would be working on for the next few months. She had told the client she would have it ready by March, but with nothing and no one standing in her way, she thought she could get the job done by mid-February.

Morgan sipped his soda as he looked over her shoulder. He had ridden his mountain bike over despite several inches of snow on the ground so he could give his moms some personal time. Jake didn't mind. She enjoyed his company.

"That's a cool one, Cousin Jake."

"I like it, too."

Even though she was proud of the design plan she had come up with, she still thought *Shy Girl* was her best work. Not surprising considering the boat had been a labor of love. It had started out as just another project, but it certainly hadn't ended up that way.

Jake began to make a list of the supplies she would need to complete her current project. When she hit the home improvement store in a few days, she might have to make two trips in order to gather everything she needed.

"How much do you think it will cost to build it?" Morgan asked.

Jake looked at the steadily growing list. "A lot, but I think the client can afford it if the size of his vacation house is any indication."

"I thought you said size doesn't matter."

She turned to look at him. "You have got to stop paying attention to every single thing I say."

Morgan grinned. "How else am I supposed to learn the fun stuff?"

"As long as you don't tell Kate and Tess where you picked it up."

"Too late. They already know." When the doorbell rang, he put his soda down and bounded toward the living room. "I'll get it."

Jake set Morgan's can of soda on a coaster and returned her attention to her blueprints. Only a salesman or a Jehovah's Witness would be out in this kind of weather. She didn't have time for either.

"Whatever they're selling, tell them I don't want any."

"Okay."

After Morgan opened the door, Jake heard him gasp as if the cold had taken his breath away.

"Cousin Jake, you'll never believe who—I mean, it's for you. Since you have company, I'm going to go home, okay?"

"Call me when you get there," Jake said reflexively.

"Okay. Bye!"

Morgan's feet thumped on the porch as he ran down the steps and grabbed his bike off the front lawn. Jake could picture him furiously churning the pedals despite the bad conditions. The roads had been salted, but Jake didn't know how quickly they would freeze up again.

"Watch out for the ice!"

Morgan always rode his bike like he was bidding to become the next Evel Knievel, extreme sports star, or both. When he didn't respond to her plea to exercise caution, Jake knew he was probably already halfway home. Knowing him, he'd make it to his driveway two streets over before she even made it to her front door.

Jake pushed herself away from the dining room table with a sigh. She had at least another hour of work to do before she reached a stopping point, but it seemed work would have to wait.

When she saw who was at the door, however, work suddenly became the last thing on her mind.

Shy stood on the porch, two large duffels at her feet. Melting snow dripped from her thickly-soled boots.

"What are you doing here?" Jake asked, trying not to read too much into Shy's unexpected presence on her doorstep.

Shy stepped toward her.

"My name's Ashley Silva. I don't know anything about relationships, but if you take a chance on me, I guarantee I will love you for the rest of my life."

Jake had fantasized about this moment for weeks, but she had never dreamed it would come to pass. Now that the moment had finally arrived, dozens of questions flooded her mind.

"How—What—" Jake was so flustered she couldn't form a complete sentence. "I don't even know where to begin," she said, admitting defeat.

Shy took another step forward, erasing the distance between them. "How about," she said as her arms slipped around Jake's neck, "with a boat ride?"

Jake welcomed Shy into her arms and back into her life. Not for a few days or a few months. Forever.

"I can't think of a better place to start."

About the Author

Yolanda Wallace is not a professional writer, but she plays one in her spare time. Her love of travel and adventure has helped her pen the globe-spanning novels *In Medias Res*, *Rum Spring*, *Lucky Loser*, the Lambda Award-winning *Month of Sundays*, and *Murphy's Law*. Her short stories have appeared in multiple anthologies including *Romantic Interludes 2: Secrets* and *Women of the Dark Streets*. She and her partner live in beautiful coastal Georgia, where they are parents to four children of the four-legged variety—a boxer and three cats.

Books Available from Bold Strokes Books

Love's Bounty by Yolanda Wallace. Lobster boat captain Jake Myers stopped living the day she cheated death, but meeting greenhorn Shy Silva stirs her back to life. (978-1-62639334-9)

Just Three Words by Melissa Brayden. Sometimes the one you want is the one you least suspect. Accountant Samantha Ennis has her ordered life disrupted when heartbreaker Hunter Blair moves into her trendy Soho loft. (978-1-62639-335-6)

Lay Down the Law by Carsen Taite. Attorney Peyton Davis returns to her Texas roots to take on big oil and the Mexican Mafia, but will her investigation thwart her chance at true love? (978-1-62639-336-3)

Playing in Shadow by Lesley Davis. Survivor's guilt threatens to keep Bryce trapped in her nightmare world unless Scarlet's love can pull her out of the darkness back into the light. (978-1-62639-337-0)

Soul Selecta by Gill McKnight. Soul mates are hell to work with. (978-1-62639-338-7)

The Revelation of Beatrice Darby by Jean Copeland. Adolescence is complicated, but Beatrice Darby is about to discover how impossible it can seem to a lesbian coming of age in conservative 1950s New England. (978-1-62639-339-4)

Twice Lucky by Mardi Alexander. For firefighter Mackenzie James and Dr. Sarah Macarthur, there's suddenly a whole lot more in life to understand, to consider, to risk…someone will need to fight for her life. (978-1-62639-325-7)

Shadow Hunt by L.L. Raand. With young to raise and her Pack under attack, Sylvan, Alpha of the wolf Weres, takes on her greatest challenge when she determines to uncover the faceless enemies known as the Shadow Lords. A Midnight Hunters novel. (978-1-62639-326-4)

Heart of the Game by Rachel Spangler. A baseball writer falls for a single mom, but can she ever love anything as much as she loves the game? (978-1-62639-327-1)

Getting Lost by Michelle Grubb. Twenty-eight days, thirteen European countries, a tour manager fighting attraction, and an accused murderer: Stella and Phoebe's journey of a lifetime begins here. (978-1-62639-328-8)

Prayer of the Handmaiden by Merry Shannon. Celibate priestess Kadrian must defend the kingdom of Ithyria from a dangerous enemy and ultimately choose between her duty to the Goddess and the love of her childhood sweetheart, Erinda. (978-1-62639-329-5)

The Witch of Stalingrad by Justine Saracen. A Soviet "night witch" pilot and American journalist meet on the Eastern Front in WW II and struggle through carnage, conflicting politics, and the deadly Russian winter. (978-1-62639-330-1)

Pedal to the Metal by Jesse J. Thoma. When unreformed thief Dubs Williams is released from prison to help Max Winters bust a car theft ring, Max learns that to catch a thief, get in bed with one. (978-1-62639-239-7)

Dragon Horse War by D. Jackson Leigh. A priestess of peace and a fiery warrior must defeat a vicious uprising that entwines their destinies and ultimately their hearts. (978-1-62639-240-3)

For the Love of Cake by Erin Dutton. When everything is on the line, and one taste can break a heart, will pastry chefs Maya and Shannon take a chance on reality? (978-1-62639-241-0)

Betting on Love by Alyssa Linn Palmer. A quiet country-girl-at-heart and a live-life-to-the-fullest biker take a risk at offering each other their hearts. (978-1-62639-242-7)

The Deadening by Yvonne Heidt. The lines between good and evil, right and wrong, have always been blurry for Shade. When Raven's actions force her to choose, which side will she come out on? (978-1-62639-243-4)

Ordinary Mayhem by Victoria A. Brownworth. Faye Blakemore has been taking photographs since she was ten, but those same photographs threaten to destroy everything she knows and everything she loves. (978-1-62639-315-8)

One Last Thing by Kim Baldwin & Xenia Alexiou. Blood is thicker than pride. The final book in the Elite Operative Series brings together foes, family, and friends to start a new order. (978-1-62639-230-4)

Songs Unfinished by Holly Stratimore. Two aspiring rock stars learn that falling in love while pursuing their dreams can be harmonious—if they can only keep their pasts from throwing them out of tune. (978-1-62639-231-1)

Beyond the Ridge by L.T. Marie. Will a contractor and a horse rancher overcome their family differences and find common ground to build a life together? (978-1-62639-232-8)

Swordfish by Andrea Bramhall. Four women battle the demons from their pasts. Will they learn to let go, or will happiness be forever beyond their grasp? (978-1-62639-233-5)

The Fiend Queen by Barbara Ann Wright. Princess Katya and her consort Starbride must turn evil against evil in order to banish Fiendish power from their kingdom, and only love will pull them back from the brink. (978-1-62639-234-2)

Up the Ante by PJ Trebelhorn. When Jordan Stryker and Ashley Noble meet again fifteen years after a short-lived affair, are either of them prepared to gamble on a chance at love? (978-1-62639-237-3)

Speakeasy by MJ Williamz. When mob leader Helen Byrne sets her sights on the girlfriend of Al Capone's right-hand man, passion and tempers flare on the streets of Chicago. (978-1-62639-238-0)

Venus in Love by Tina Michele. Morgan Blake can't afford any distractions and Ainsley Dencourt can't afford to lose control—but the beauty of life and art usually lies in the unpredictable strokes of the artist's brush. (978-1-62639-220-5)

Rules of Revenge by AJ Quinn. When a lethal operative on a collision course with her past agrees to help a CIA analyst on a critical assignment, the encounter proves explosive in ways neither woman anticipated. (978-1-62639-221-2)

The Romance Vote by Ali Vali. Chili Alexander is a sought-after campaign consultant who isn't prepared when her boss's daughter, Samantha Pellegrin, comes to work at the firm and shakes up Chili's life from the first day. (978-1-62639-222-9)

Advance: Exodus Book One by Gun Brooke. Admiral Dael Caydoc's mission to find a new homeworld for the Oconodian people is hazardous, but working with the infuriating Commander Aniwyn "Spinner" Seclan endangers her heart and soul. (978-1-62639-224-3)

UnCatholic Conduct by Stevie Mikayne. Jil Kidd goes under-cover to investigate fraud at St. Marguerite's Catholic School, but life gets complicated when her student is killed—and she begins to fall for her prime target. (978-1-62639-304-2)

Season's Meetings by Amy Dunne. Catherine Birch reluctantly ventures on the festive road trip from hell with beautiful stranger Holly Daniels only to discover the road to true love has its own obstacles to maneuver. (978-1-62639-227-4)

Myth and Magic: Queer Fairy Tales edited by Radclyffe and Stacia Seaman. Myth, magic, and monsters—the stuff of childhood dreams (or nightmares) and adult fantasies. (978-1-62639-225-0)

Nine Nights on the Windy Tree by Martha Miller. Recovering drug addict, Bertha Brannon, is an attorney who is trying to stay clean when a murder sends her back to the bad end of town. (978-1-62639-179-6)

Driving Lessons by Annameekee Hesik. Dive into Abbey Brooks's sophomore year as she attempts to figure out the amazing, but sometimes complicated, life of a you-know-who girl at Gila High School. (978-1-62639-228-1)

Asher's Shot by Elizabeth Wheeler. Asher Price's candid photographs capture the truth, but when his success requires exposing an enemy, Asher discovers his only shot at happiness involves revealing secrets of his own. (978-1-62639-229-8)

Courtship by Carsen Taite. Love and justice—a lethal mix or a perfect match? (978-1-62639-210-6)

Against Doctor's Orders by Radclyffe. Corporate financier Presley Worth wants to shut down Argyle Community Hospital, but Dr. Harper Rivers will fight her every step of the way, if she can also fight their growing attraction. (978-1-62639-211-3)

A Spark of Heavenly Fire by Kathleen Knowles. Kerry and Beth are building their life together, but unexpected circumstances could destroy their happiness. (978-1-62639-212-0)

Never Too Late by Julie Blair. When Dr. Jamie Hammond is forced to hire a new office manager, she's shocked to come face to face with Carla Grant and memories from her past. (978-1-62639-213-7)

Widow by Martha Miller. Judge Bertha Brannon must solve the murder of her lover, a policewoman she thought she'd grow old with. As more bodies pile up, the murderer starts coming for her. (978-1-62639-214-4)

Twisted Echoes by Sheri Lewis Wohl. What's a woman to do when she realizes the voices in her head are real? (978-1-62639-215-1)

Criminal Gold by Ann Aptaker. Through a dangerous night in New York in 1949, Cantor Gold, dapper dyke-about-town, smuggler of fine art, is forced by a crime lord to be his instrument of vengeance. (978-1-62639-216-8)

The Melody of Light by M.L. Rice. After surviving abuse and loss, will Riley Gordon be able to navigate her first year of college and accept true love and family? (978-1-62639-219-9)

Because of You by Julie Cannon. What would you do for the woman you were forced to leave behind? (978-1-62639-199-4)

The Job by Jove Belle. Sera always dreamed that she would one day reunite with Tor. She just didn't think it would involve terrorists, firearms, and hostages. (978-1-62639-200-7)

Making Time by C.J. Harte. Two women going in different directions meet after fifteen years and struggle to reconnect in spite of the past that separated them. (978-1-62639-201-4)

Once The Clouds Have Gone by KE Payne. Overwhelmed by the dark clouds of her past, Tag Grainger is lost until the intriguing and spirited Freddie Metcalfe unexpectedly forces her to reevaluate her life. (978-1-62639-202-1)